TANYA E WILLIAMS

BECOMING

MRS.

SMITH

THE *Smith Family* SERIES

BOOK ONE

Printed in the United States of America
Published by Rippling Effects
Surrey, British Columbia, Canada www.ripplingeffects.ca

Visit the author's website at www.tanyaewilliams.com

FIRST EDITION
Cover Design by Ana Grigoriu
Paperback ISBN: 978-1-775-070-60-3
EPub ISBN: 978-1-775-070-64-1
Kindle ISBN: 978-1-775-070-63-4
Audiobook ISBN: 978-1-775-070-61-0

For Mom,
Who taught me that courage, like love, often resides in the thread
of daily life. Have the courage to choose who you want to be and
begin the act of becoming it.
Without you, none of this would have been possible.
With utmost gratitude,
Love, Tanya

GET YOUR FREE COPY OF

AT THE CORNER OF FICTION & HISTORY - FACTS & FOLLIES THAT INSPIRE THE STORIES

To instantly receive a complimentary eBook copy of At The Corner of Fiction & History sign up for Tanya E Williams' Free author newsletter at www.tanyaewilliams.com

✳ ✳ ✳

 ebruary 1935

THE WALLS of the old farmhouse quiver. Thump. Thump. Thump. The sound reverberates inside of me with each strike against our solid oak door. My insides shake like a ground tremor. Until now, I couldn't have believed my body could shake any more brutally. This cruel and ruthless fever has vibrated inside of me since before yesterday's sunrise. Doc Walton and his hammer, the cause of all the commotion, have traveled from Cedar Springs. He has since confirmed Mother's fears. Scarlet fever has attacked our home and invaded my slight, now fragile body. The notice nailed to the front door is both a proclamation of quarantine and a warning. Those who enter or leave the Sanderson property will be reported and punished by South Dakota law.

At eleven years old, I'm not keen to lift my nightdress for the doctor. Mother's stern gaze, which bores through me from the corner of the bedroom I share with Iris, tells me refusing is not an option. My skin, warm to the touch, shivers as air whispers across the tiny red bumps. The doctor listens to my heart with his instrument, the round metal end cold from winter frost, before he lowers my bedclothes and tucks me into bed. He murmurs to himself as he pats my shoulder and smiles sadly, before the latch on his black bag snaps shut.

Mother follows close behind him. He tosses into the fire the slender piece of smooth, pale wood he pressed against my tongue. Mother closes the bedroom door to their muffled voices.

Exhaustion overwhelms me, and I sink deeper under the weighted quilts, seeking warmth and stillness for my unsettled body. Father's deep voice, even at a whisper, echoes through my window. I hear him and the doctor speaking, despite the thick layer of fabric Mother has placed over the glass to shield the room from light and cold. Their hushed voices sound serious, and their words drift over the front porch to my red hot ears.

Without a doubt, I am ill. Even if I survive the fever, the doctor worries about the strain on my heart. I bury myself deeper in the heavy cocoon of blankets while my warm breath heats the darkened sanctuary. Tinges of despair overcome me. Fear, instead of fever, ushers in a fresh vibration that leaves my body in a tangled heap of shivers.

I demand my body to heal. First I pray, and then I negotiate. If I could somehow put more love in my heart, perhaps it would grow strong again. I promise to do all my chores without complaint for the rest of my life. I will be patient with Iris, even when she makes me want to scream. I will never roll my eyes at Mother for as long as I live.

Before sleep descends over me again, I plead with God to make me well. I promise to live a simple life. I will never wish for extravagance, if only He will save me from the fever.

*P*erhaps the absence of everyday life makes my dreams so vivid, so real. Or maybe my mind is protecting me from the horrors of my illness, desperately attempting to experience life again. Mother says, with a sternness that makes all other explanations vanish, that the fever is the only cause of my hallucinations. Either way, I dream as if I am living in full color.

The tall grassy fields sway in a gentle breeze. Stems rustle against one another as if sharing secrets. The springtime flowers tilt their petals toward the sky, and I feel warm sunshine kiss my face. John Smith, the kindest person I have ever known, sits before me with a gentle, lopsided smile.

John and I sit on the front steps of our one room school. A breeze brushes the hair away from my face. The spring air ignites a sense of comfort in my weary skin.

As the two oldest students at school, the teacher sent us outside to talk through math problems that have stumped us all morning, while the others study for the upcoming spelling bee. I read the first problem aloud as John scribbles notes. Puzzled by the word problem, I reread it slowly. John, pencil readied at his paper, pauses and chuckles.

"What is so funny?" I ask, brow furrowed in concentration.

"You tucked your hair behind your ear." He laughs, and his free hand slaps his thigh in mock hilarity.

I hesitate before responding. "Okay?" I raise an eyebrow while he grins at me.

"I know when you're ready to get serious," he says. "You tuck your hair behind your right ear, like a tell. You know, whenever you are about to focus on an important task, you always tuck your hair."

"No I don't." My voice conveys a weak annoyance and a slight embarrassment. I extract the swatch of hair from behind my ear and nervously smooth the strand against my scalp.

John's laughter transforms into a sweet smile. He reaches out a hand and slides a blond, wavy strand behind my ear. His hand touches my cheek for the briefest moment. He blushes. "Father was teaching me about tells is all, Vi. You know, like with animals. Making sure I could handle that mean old bull that wanders all over the county in case we stumble across his path. So I started to watch people, too, and I noticed you put your hair behind your ear every time we work on math problems."

I return his smile with a shy one of my own. I lower my eyes and feel my cheeks grow warm from his attention and his bold admission of watching me.

"Violet. Violet. Wake up, dear."

The world moves backward and forward. Why is the world in motion? No, the world isn't shaking. Through the fogginess of a rooted sleep, I recognize Mother's voice. She pulls me from the depths of blackness with a jerk. I feel as if I have only slept a few moments before she cruelly wrenches me from the veil of my coma.

"Violet. You must wake up."

I lift my eyelids a fraction. The act feels as arduous as when I attempted to lift that old yoke onto Bud, the tallest of Daddy's horses. Light penetrates my eyes like a hot poker and I squeeze them shut.

"Violet," Mother pleads. "You've been asleep for two days."

"What?" I groan and roll away from the hands clenching my shoulders.

Never one to dismiss a task she has set her mind to, Mother steps around my bed in three swift motions. She settles herself into the small space between my elbows and knees, while I lie in a fetal position.

"Drink," she commands. "Now, Violet." She holds a small metal cup in front of me. Her determination is embodied in her stiff posture, but worry lays creased across her forehead.

Her worry, not her determination, coerces me to prop myself onto my elbows. I tilt my head as she places the cup to my mouth. Warm milk cuts across my swollen, cracked lips before assaulting my throat and trickling down to the sharp knives that feel lodged there.

"That's better." Mother runs her palm over my bedratted hair.

"Two days?" Grogginess fills my voice, and I return my head to the pillow. The milk meanders down to my vacant stomach and gurgles.

She nods quickly and turns her face away in an effort to hide her moist eyes.

I manage a raspy response, my voice laced with fatigue. "How long have I been here? In bed, I mean."

"We've been quarantined for over three weeks now."

"I don't remember."

"Nature's way." She shrugs. "You are better off not to remember." She smiles tightly, a tinge of relief in her sunken eyes. I realize that, while I have been submerged in a deep sleep for weeks, Mother hasn't slept at all.

I tuck a damp, tangled strand of hair behind my ear. Her love ignites my desire to find the strength to survive this illness. I silently promise to follow Mother's instructions, each and every one of them.

***

*A*pril 1935

YESTERDAY, Doc Walton lifted the quarantine from the farm. Father wasted no time. He pulled the warning sign off our front door with his bare hands before running toward the one posted on the fence. The doctor listens to my heart and confirms the existence of permanent damage. With a sullen face, I retreat to the comfort of my bed. Mother leads the doctor to the front room, pummelling him with questions about my life and future health.

I lie with my back facing the open door and hug my chest. My lip quivers as I try to hold back hot tears. I feel damaged. I used to have a strong heart. A kind heart. A heart that was full of joy, spilling over with abundance. Will others see a spoiled heart? Father always says how natural I am with the horses. Will they sense a difference in me? Will I love as well as I used to? What if I have to live with Mother and Father forever? A spinster, like Miss Mabel, whom everyone tolerates at church gatherings. Perhaps she, too, has a weak heart. Blood thumps in my ears as I glimpse the life I might lead with this irreparable heart. Grief and sleep consume me as thoughts of my future life percolate in my overcrowded consciousness.

I wake to the low vibration of the wooden rocking chair. The runners scuff the wood floor with each forward tilt. The room is dark except the flicker of the front room fire casting shadows on the bedroom wall. I remain still, not wanting to talk with Mother, who I know from experience is the occupant of the rocker.

My stillness does not fool her. The rocker squeaks as she rises and positions herself at the foot of my bed.

"Violet, I understand you are upset, and I won't pretend to understand how you are feeling." She rubs my foot. "It's a miracle you survived at all, and for that, we need be grateful."

"Grateful! You want me to be grateful?" I spit out the words as I bolt up to face her. "I am never going to be well again. Don't you see? I am ruined. My life is over. I should have died from the fever. I could have saved you all the trouble."

"What trouble?" Mother's hand is firm around my foot, like an anchor.

"Nobody will love someone with half a heart. Why would they? I could die at any moment. Nobody wants to risk loving someone they are going to lose." My shoulders shake as the rising panic forces out wails of despair.

Mother moves closer and wraps her arms around me. We sit cradled together as my convulsions dwindle into weary hiccups.

"You are not broken. Not like you think, Violet. You know, I don't often speak about my father. He was a good man, a strong man. He used to sit me on his knee each night after dinner and tell me stories. Oh, how the man could coax a tale into life." Mother laughs at the memory. She pulls away to look me in the eye. "I loved him more than I can say, and he left us far too early." Her eyes are rimmed with moisture. "But I can tell you without a doubt that even if I had known he would leave us so soon, I wouldn't have loved him less. I would have loved him even more. The state of your heart doesn't change who you are. You are Violet, and you are worthy of being loved. I love you and, no matter what, I always will."

I want to ask questions. The desire to know more about Mother and her family burns inside me. I never met my grandparents or my mother's brother. All I know is that Grandfather and Uncle Joe died in a barn fire, trying to save the livestock, and that Grandmother, rumor has it, died of a broken heart.

After a long embrace and a kiss goodnight, Mother tucks me into bed. She sings a soft lullaby as she places the quilt from the rocker over my legs, and she closes the door behind her.

Mother's words rattle around in my head for what feels like an eternity. If I cannot repair my weakened heart, I will have to make myself more lovable. I can do that. I can be more caring, more considerate, more patient. I can be more responsible and hardworking. I may not be the storyteller my grandfather was, but I can be what others need me to be. Then they will have no choice but to love me. "Violet," I tell myself, "time for you to grow up. No more childish games. You must be a responsible young woman."

I vow to live by my newly constructed plan, and before sleep takes my hand and quiets my mind, I make my first step toward maturity. I bow my head to thank God for saving me from the fever.

***

July 1935

SUMMER DAYS in South Dakota are the kind you want to bottle and save. This summer feels extra sweet, given the months of confinement in my bedroom. Classes finished in late June, and Miss Marshall was impressed by my effort, enough to pass me to the next grade. My strength improves each day, and I can finally help Mother with the garden. Iris flits around, chasing butterflies and inspecting ladybugs while I crouch among the strawberry plants. Mother hums a church hymn as she moves between rows, adding sweet red berries to her basket.

"How old were you when your mother died?" I hold my breath in anticipation and tilt my head toward the bush to avoid eye contact.

"I was fourteen." Mother stands and stretches her back, sneaking a glance in my direction. "Why do you ask?"

I shrug and tread with care. "I guess I've always wondered what your life was like before you had us."

Her large brimmed hat casts a shadow over her face. I can't read her expression. "Do you have a particular question in mind?"

"Well, I was curious if Grandmother really did die of a broken heart. I've been wondering if it's contagious. You know, like how Iris and I have blond wavy hair, same as yours."

Mother's dirtstained hand covers her mouth as she giggles. "Oh, Violet. Honey, a broken heart isn't passed down through generations." She tilts her head to the side. "Are you worried you inherited my mother's broken heart? Is that what is troubling you?"

A solemn nod is all I can offer, for fear of dissolving into a puddle of raw emotion. I've tried to be grownup about the situation, but my weak heart won't give my mind any peace. I've started to wonder if a weak heart and a broken heart are similar in nature. Perhaps I will die of a broken heart, after all.

"Come now." Mother puts her arm around my shoulders and pulls me closer. "My mother died of a broken heart. That is true but not in the way you think. She wasn't sick. She couldn't live with the loss of my father and brother." A furrow develops across her forehead, and I imagine she's traveling through childhood memories. "She was a good woman, a loving mother. Sometimes, life gets the better of us. That is why I urge you to embrace each moment. Find joy in the simple aspects of your life. You can't always control what happens, but you can choose how you react."

Mother holds me at arm's length and lowers her face to mine. The brim of her hat touches the top of my head, shielding our faces from the garden. "Your heart, however, is not broken. You are in no danger of dying from a broken heart. I can promise you that, Violet."

I revisit Mother's words every time my heart flutters in my chest. They comfort me as I become familiar with the new rhythm of my heart. I remain cautious, though, not running or jumping like Iris does—free and with reckless abandon. I keep my promise to myself, and with consistent daily fortitude, I mold myself into a young woman like a caterpillar molds itself into a butterfly.

As I gain confidence in my body's ability, I help Father with the horses. The first time I visit the barn, I am reassured. The horses don't notice my heart isn't the same as before. They welcome me with nuzzles and snorts. I take this as a good sign, as I know how sensitive these beautiful creatures can be. My determination to live a full and happy life is renewed as they crunch the carrots I've brought from the garden.

Summer days are busy on the farm. There is always a field to plow or hay to bail in preparation for winter. Father busies himself mending, building, and painting, in addition to his regular work. Caring for the garden, the vegetables that will feed us through winter, takes precedence over leisure time on every good weather day.

With school closed for the summer, church on Sundays is the only scheduled time we gather with friends. Sundays make long summer days worth the effort. The sweet tea tastes sweeter. The fried chicken is crispier. And we treasure the time with friends and neighbors. The adults gather on blankets in the shade, and the young children chase one another in a disorganized game of tag.

At eleven, with a birthday next month, I find myself lost between age groups. The adults' conversation still borders on dull, but I've grown out of the children's makebelieve.

John and I sit on the church steps as he tries to teach me how to make a whistle out of a long blade of grass, a skill I have yet to master. "What does your heart feel like now?" John tugs at the blade of grass. "Mother said the fever got you good. She's been praying for you since she got word."

I smile at the thought of John's mother including me in their evening prayers. John's kindness comes from deep within the Smith family. "You know when you're pulling a wagon but one of the wheels isn't quite right?"

"I think so."

"Kind of like that. Like a catch. That wheel makes the pulling harder. The wagon still moves, but there is a lag to the rhythm that makes it feel a little uneven."

John's head bobs. "I see what you are saying. So your heart doesn't hurt you, then?"

"No. There is no pain, just a restless feeling, like butterflies filling up my chest. At first I thought my heart was broken." I look away to hide my insecurity about the state of my heart. "But Mother is certain that isn't the case."

"I don't suspect your heart is broken either, Vi." John leans his shoulder into mine, capturing my attention. "I like you all the same anyway."

A wide smile spreads across my face before a laugh escapes, releasing with it any worry about John and my weak heart.

***

 ctober 1935

AUTUMN SWEEPS in with a crisp breeze, snuffing out any remnants of summer. Fall colors decorate the landscape as the low sun casts a golden glow across the fields. The air is thick with the scent of fires. Farmers burn foliage and brush as the leaves crinkle and fall.

Mother and I have been pulling in the garden for weeks. Each Saturday, we spend hours canning, drying, and storing vegetables. The cellar is almost full, which is a welcome sight. I would much rather be in the garden than over a hot stove. Last week, we cleared the apples from the tree and the ground, which resulted in jars filled to the brim with apple preserves. As this morning's frost threatens to blanket the ground with icy crystals, Mother and I gather the remaining root vegetables and squashes and prepare them for storage.

Iris lugs her overgrown pumpkin to the back steps and waits impatiently for Father to help her carve it in time for Halloween. She announced last night at dinner that she plans to dress up as a cat this year, so when she's not pacing in front of her pumpkin, she's practicing her "meow" for the big day.

Mother, tired of listening to the strangled pretend cat sounds, closes the kitchen window in exasperation. Within minutes, the window is laced with steam from the bubbling canning pot. The final batch of jars is nestled in the pot as I collect the discarded vegetable bits for the chicken coop.

I head out the back door, arms full of the metal bowl heaped high with scraps. The fresh air washes over me, soothing my red hot face.

"When is Father going to carve my pumpkin?" Iris asks as I make my way down the steps.

"Did you ask him if he could help you with the pumpkin today?" Iris squats beside her pumpkin. "Can you ask him?" She looks up at me with a hopeful gaze. "I want the big ol' jack-o'-lantern smile to go right here." She tilts the pumpkin back and points.

"I will see if he's in the barn, but Iris, Halloween isn't for another week. Father may want you to wait a bit longer."

A small pout forms across her lips. "Please, ask him. He won't say no to you."

"We'll see." I turn away from her and continue toward the barn.

"Hey, Bud," I say to my favorite of Daddy's horses as I walk by his stall. His chestnut nose sticks out to greet me. "I'll be back. Give me a minute." He whinnies in response as his head bobs up and down.

"You're the only one I know who actually gets an answer from that stubborn old beast." Father chuckles as he steps out of an empty stall, broom in hand.

I laugh, but I know it is true. The animals and I understand one another.

"Let me help you with that, darlin'." Father takes the bowl from my arms and vanishes behind the barn's back door to dump the load into the chicken feed.

I stroll back to Bud and scratch his ear before planting a kiss on his nose. I move the hair from between his eyes and reveal the white star atop his forehead. "You're a good boy, aren't you?"

Father returns from the chicken coop and hands me the empty bowl. "All finished with the garden?"

"That was the last batch. Good thing, too. There isn't a shred of room left in the cellar."

"Mighty fine news, that is. Enough to get us through to next summer, I presume." Father nods and reaches for the broom.

A shiver takes hold of me. I begin to retreat to the warm kitchen when I remember. "Iris is waiting on the back steps for you. She has her heart set on carving her pumpkin tonight."

"Does she, now?" Father rubs his chin. "Guess I best be getting done with this sweeping so I don't disappoint. Tell her we will carve after dinner, but she'll have to help Mother with the dinner dishes first."

"She will be delighted." I smile at his willingness to please her, but as I walk away, I wonder if Iris was right. Maybe I am the one he would never tell no.

* * *

 uly 1936

THE HEAT SMOLDERS in the stagnant sky. Sweat trickles down the side of my face as I fill pails of water for the livestock. The past few days have been hotter than most. "A record high," the stern voice on the radio said during last night's broadcast. Mother and I have been working to keep the garden moist and the animals watered. Even Iris has become listless in the extreme heat. She lounges in the shade of the back porch, her doll perched on her lap. Father is consumed with rebuilding the pig enclosure, after a neighbor rescued one of our biggest pigs wandering toward town.

I am filling another pail for the horse trough when a shadow appears near my feet.

"Hey, Vi." John's hands are stuffed into his trouser pockets, and his face is flushed with heat.

"John. What brings you by?" I brush aside the damp hair, stuck to my face. "Little warm for a walk in the country, don't you think?"

He laughs as he removes his cap and pushes his own damp hair back across the top of his head before replacing the cap. "Father said to come by and offer help with the pig pen.

"That is awful kind of you." I feel my cheeks warm but console myself with the knowledge that they are already red from the sun. "Father is around back. I'll take you there." I leave the pail beneath the spigot and wipe my hands on the back of my dress.

We enter the shady barn, filled with pigs' noise, unhappy to be in the warm, confined space. When my eyes finally adjust to the darkness, I notice John glancing sideways at me. My eyes meet his and he gives me a lopsided half smile. My tummy flips in response.

"Maybe when I'm done here, we could go put our feet in the stream to cool off," John says as he holds the door open for me.

"I'll have to check with Mother. Iris will want to come, too." Apology edges into my voice.

"Sure. Iris is welcome, too."

We step into the brightness, and I shade my eyes with my hand. I

spot Father bent over a low section of fence, knees planted in the dry, crusty soil. "The cavalry is here," I call out to him.

"John." Father stands and extends his hand for John to shake. "Nice to see you, son."

"John's come to help with the fence."

"Mighty thoughtful of you, John." Father beams at him as he wipes sweat from his forehead.

"I'll let you two get at it." I walk back toward the barn, unable to hide my smile. I know that although John was gracious enough to invite Iris to the stream, his invitation was clearly intended for me.

***

$\mathcal{M}$ arch 1937

EASTER DOESN'T SUIT the month of March in South Dakota. Rain, sleet, and snow still frequent Cedar Springs often enough to make the town just plain messy. I struggle to welcome spring flowers and sunny days before winter has made its departure. Yet, here we are, huddled together for warmth in the church pews, celebrating both the ascension of Jesus into Heaven and the beginning of spring. Iris shivers between Mother and me, too vain to put on her winter coat and cover the new dress Mother sewed. The heat inside the church doesn't cut through the frostiness, and I notice my breath forming clouds as I sing along with the hymn.

During the potluck after the service, we share a meal with our friends and neighbors. Since the weather is too sour to eat outside, the men position the pews against the side walls to free the floor space for folding chairs and tables. We bow our heads in thanks. Many families are struggling in the low economy, which makes the Easter celebration even more meaningful. Everyone is welcome to enjoy the food and festivities.

Father and Reverend Campbell discuss the *Farmers' Almanac*, both wishing for an early spring. John sneaks into the seat beside me, his plate heaped full of mashed potatoes, green beans, and baked ham.

"Did you hear the news?" John asks between mouthfuls.

"What news?" I cast him a questioning look as I move the green beans around my plate.

"Miss Marshall," he says. "She's getting married."

"Does that mean we'll have to call her Mrs. Marshall?" Iris asks from across the table.

"No, Iris. She will have a new last name. She will take the last name of her new husband."

"Huh?" Iris looks dumbfounded.

"Say Violet marries me." John hesitates and casts me a brief glance. "She would become Mrs. Smith."

"Oh! I get it." Iris's eyes light up, and John focuses on the food before him. Iris prattles on, wondering aloud what Miss Marshall's new name will be as John gathers his composure.

I lean toward him and whisper into his ear, "Good example. She understands now."

John doesn't look my way, but I see a faint upward turn of the corner of his mouth.

✳✳✳

 ugust 1938

"THIS ISN'T FAIR." I stand before Mother, arms crossed. "I am ready to move up a grade. Miss Marshall, I mean Mrs. Graham, said so herself."

"This isn't about fair, Violet." Mother sits on the back porch, rocking in the shade as she darns a pair of Father's socks.

"Iris shouldn't make decisions about my education."

"Iris isn't making any decision," Mother scoffs. "Your father and I feel that three years at high school will be plenty of time for your education." Mother stares at me with a quiet steadfastness, daring me to argue.

I clench my fists and take a deep breath. "I understand that Iris wants me to stay. Really, I do. I am excited about this opportunity is all. Going to high school this September would be good for me."

"Violet, your father and I insist that you continue at the country school for one more year." Mother sighs, and the sock and needles fall to her lap. "Iris, isn't the only one who isn't quite ready for you to go."

"I'd be home every weekend," I say, though the weight of my message is deflated by the realization that Mother still worries for me and my weakened heart.

Mother's voice softens. "Your father and I have agreed to next year. I promise to permit you to enter high school next September."

"Fine." My reply is laced with disdain, and I cringe as I hurl the word. I turn on my heel and walk down the porch steps, away from the conversation.

I kick at the stones embedded in the driveway. I felt such pride when Mrs. Graham delivered the news that I had been accepted into the high school program a year early. I was honored, especially since I had made up so much work after being sick. I ran all the way home, Iris calling after me the entire way. Excitement won out over ladylike behavior as I burst into the kitchen to tell Mother the good news. I should have known then, by her strained look of terror, masked by a tight smile. I shouldn't have gotten my hopes up. Disappointment engulfs me as I head down the shaded path toward the stream.

Sunlight filters through the dense leaves of the trees lining the dirt path. I hear water rushing over the rocks, smooth from years of erosion. I step out from the shade and slip off my shoes and socks, feeling the coolness of the dark, firm soil. A splash catches my ear, and I look up stream to see John surrounded by several large boulders, standing in knee deep water with his trousers rolled up. He holds a fishing pole in one hand as his other guides the line, his eyes fixed on where the line enters the water.

I watch as he moves the line back and forth before I decide to make myself known. "Hello, John."

His head snaps up, and he stumbles among the boulders and the fast moving water. "Hi, Vi." He waves. "Be right there."

I settle myself on the bank, close to the water's edge, and dangle my feet into the refreshing rapids until he meanders back to shore.

"Catch anything?" I ask as he sets down his fishing pole and sits beside me.

"Just numb feet." He shrugs. "Always best to get out here in the morning or as the sun is setting."

"I don't think I'd be too good at fishing. Not enough patience, I'm afraid."

"Aw, I don't know about that. Takes focus more than patience." John's eyes never leave the rippling waters. "Didn't expect to see you out here, especially without Iris in tow."

"I needed to get away for a while is all. Be alone with my thoughts."

John picks at the fuzzy end of a tall piece of grass. "I'd say you've come to the right place. I come here for the quiet and to think." He pauses before adding, "And to fish. Something bothering you, Vi?"

"Mother and I had a disagreement."

"That'll happen." John's statement of the obvious catches me off guard.

"Yes. Yes, I suppose so." I rummage through my thoughts, attempting to speak my mind without disrespecting my parents. "I have been informed that I won't be going to high school next month, after all."

"Hmm, and this upsets you?"

"I was honored to be invited." I'm unable to conceal my righteous tone.

"I'm sure you were."

"You don't think I should be disappointed?" I can't believe I've found myself in another argument regarding the same topic.

"Well, in this situation, either you or I would be disappointed. And this time, I prefer it be you."

"What are you talking about, John Smith? Your riddles are infuriating." My back becomes rigid with indignation, and I contemplate finding another quiet spot to brood.

"If you go to high school, I won't get to see you every day, Vi." John tilts his head in my direction, and a smile curves the corners of his mouth. "That doesn't suit me, you see."

With so few words, John has managed to melt my anger and disappointment. I shake my head and smile, before kicking my feet hard against the water's edge to splash him.

✳ ✳ ✳

une 1939

THE SCREEN DOOR slaps against the frame, signaling Iris is coming to find me in the back garden. I hear Mother issue cross words from the kitchen, but at ten years old, her delight precedes her common sense. She's already moving on toward her next adventure.

"Violet." Iris sounds exasperated. "Where are you?"

I stand, and knees stained with dark prairie soil peek out from beneath my summer dress. I brush my hands against each other and dirt falls to the ground. I watch her skip toward me. She is the embodiment of a free spirit, not a care in the world and often without a thought ahead of where she stands. I giggle at her exuberance for life and embrace her in a quick hug. I hope the contagious youthfulness mixed with a touch of tomboy remains constant throughout her life.

"Can I help?"

"Of course. Though I thought you had to help Father water the pigs."

"Oh! I forgot." She dashes off toward the barn as Daddy comes 'round the corner, in search of his helper.

"I'll be back," she hollers over her shoulder, waving wildly.

Hands on his hips, Father's grim look of disappointment dissolves into a softer expression as Iris runs past him, in search of the pig pen behind the barn. I wave at him and his smile widens. He shakes his head with a laugh as he follows his youngest daughter on one of her many escapades.

I focus my attention back to the row. Bees buzz about while I weed and tend to the plants. I breathe in the earthy scent and thank God once again for the farm life. Even with tough times all around us, the farm is a constant, steady supplier of food, purpose, and sanity. I expect I would miss this place even if I had never been here.

My heart flutters, an everyday sensation since the fever. At first, the flutters filled me with dread. I spent months lamenting my weak heart. After much consternation on my part, Father, forever the optimist, suggested I view the butterflies as a message of good fortune. He insisted they exist to remind me that all is right with my body.

I tell myself all is well as I kneel to examine the strawberry plants. My mind drifts to a time, not long ago, when Mother worked beside me in the garden. She would tell stories passed down by her father while she taught me how to grow the tallest green beans and the juiciest tomatoes. Mother's soft spot for the garden was evident in the way she would glide from plant to bush. I loved watching her move between the rows. She made me feel like I was in the audience of a masterful play. Two summers ago, she entrusted me with all the garden duties, a chore I welcomed with gratitude. The time has come, though, to pass that information down to Iris before I move on to further my education in town next September. I am giddy with anticipation.

"I'm back." Her breath is labored as she halts a mere inch from the potato plants.

I notice her wet shoes, already caked with mud, and make a mental note to wash them off before she goes into the house. "You can start at that end." I point to the row opposite me. "Our job today is to pull weeds."

"Aww, really? I thought you were gonna be more fun." Her disappointment contorts her face into a large pout.

"We can have fun," I say with a forced brightness. "This is an important part of being a master gardener. You know you need to learn all about the process so you can help Mother next spring."

Iris steps over the row of strawberries and sits in the dirt. She sighs as she pulls and examines each weed before stretching with great embellishment to dispense the clump into the weed bucket. "Why do you have to go, anyway?"

"We've been over this." I measure the impatience in my voice so I don't upset her. We've already had teary discussions by the bucketful.

"The only way I can extend my education is to move to the high school in town. You know I should have gone last year. This is the right time. Iris, my education is important to me and to Mother and Father, and I want to graduate from high school."

"But why can't you get Mrs. Graham to teach you more?" Her voice climbs an octave, nibbling at the edge of a whiny tone.

"Mrs. Graham doesn't teach older students." I choose my words with care. "I know this is difficult for you to understand, but you will move to town, too, when you are older, and you will go to the high school same as me. You can be a nurse or an artist or whatever you want to be when you graduate."

Her silent sulk feels louder than the echo of chirping birds in the apple tree. "You get to have the bedroom all to yourself." I hope to boost her spirits. "You can put all your own drawings on the walls to decorate. Iris, consider the possibilities, the entire room covered with your masterpieces."

A small smile lifts the cheeks of her bowed head. "As long as you're not moving because of John." She draws out his name sarcastically. "His sisters told me their family bought a house in town. They'll attend school in Cedar Springs come September."

I stifle a smirk. "I would attend high school whether John Smith moved to town or not." I try to convey a casual, nonchalant tone, but somehow the words escape my lips sounding strangled and almost embarrassed.

Iris laughs as she rolls in the dirt. She clutches her stomach, without the slightest awareness that she has almost crushed the row of beets behind her.

I roll my eyes, trying to hide my true pleasure at the situation, and direct my attention to the swatch of weeds.

* * *

*S*eptember 1939

THE SUMMER HEAT warms the brick school house. The third week of classes end, and teachers usher us out of the stuffy building as they board up the windows in preparation of the weekend. I pause on the front steps and reposition my books for the walk back to the boarding house, where I live with other girls my age from farms surrounding Cedar Springs.

"Hi, Vi," says a soft voice.

"John. How nice to see you." I wear what I hope is my most cheerful smile.

He shuffles his feet as we walk toward the street, his eyes focused on the ground. I wonder if he would rather be somewhere else.

"I—I've seen you 'round school a few times." He pauses, and I become aware that this is the first time I have seen shyness in John Smith. "But you were always surrounded by people. You seem to have settled in at school."

I nod and wait for him to say more. When he doesn't, we stroll in silence for several blocks. The thought of a missed opportunity would kill me, so I muster up my courage. I tighten my grip on my books to help steady my nerves and ask, "John, are you being coy or has the Cedar Springs water made you nervous around me?" Little about my question could be mistaken as ambiguous, a trait I inherited from Mother.

"I've been thinking is all." He kicks at the dirt, rising a cloud of dust above his shoes. "Aw shucks, Vi. I've been thinking about you all summer and I wonder if you would see fit to go with me?" His cheeks turn rosy pink as his eyes dart about, avoiding contact with mine.

"Go with you where?" I tease. I allow him to squirm a minute before I let him off the hook. I reach for his hand and fit it into my own.

✳ ✳ ✳

ecember 1939

THE CHRISTMAS SEASON ignites a sense of magic within me. Christmas bells adorn shop doors, ringing cheerfully as customers come and go. Store windows display pretty ribbon wrapped gifts, while the bakery offers sweet breads and gingerbread men piped with frosting.

Excitement bubbles inside me as John, Helen, and I— bundled in our winter coats—leave school on our first holiday break. The past few weeks have required lots of study time, but with our tests behind us, we are free to participate in the holiday joy.

John ducks inside the bakery where his father works to purchase three gingerbread cookies, one for each of us. The warm, soft cookie almost melts in my mouth as the sweet frosting tickles my tongue.

We stand near the town center, eating our treats and listening to the carolers sing holiday favorites. A few flakes begin to fall. We lift our faces to the clouded sky and attempt to catch a few on our tongues before John walks us the rest of the way to the boarding house.

Helen says goodbye and thanks John for the cookie before she steps

inside the tall building. I imagine her retreating to the seclusion of our shared bedroom.

"You'll come for dinner?" John stuffs his hands into his jacket pockets.

The invitation for dinner came last week. Our first dinner at the Smith house as a couple. "Sunday after Christmas," I say. "Is there a dish I should bring?"

John shakes his head. "Mother already has everything planned. She was so excited you said yes. I gather this will be the best New Year's we've had yet."

"I'm looking forward to the evening."

John shivers against the cold. "I better be off. I'll see you at church. Merry Christmas, Vi."

"Merry Christmas, John." I put a hand on his shoulder, then lean in and place my lips to his cheek.

His hand touches his cheek where my lips were. "Bye."

I smile to myself as my heart flutters in my chest.

✳ ✳ ✳

*J*anuary 1940

HELEN LISTENS RAPTLY to my stories of New Year's Eve at the Smith house a week ago. I ramble about the dinner and the party hats and the banging of pots and pans at midnight. My cheeks ache from the wide smile.

"What a night." Helen collapses backward onto the bed in an exaggerated dreamy fashion. Her red hair fans out, vibrant against the white sheets. "Tell me about the kiss again."

I tuck my legs under me and lean against the head of my bed.

"When the clock struck twelve, John and I were sitting on the front porch steps. The chime sounded and John turned to look at me. He took my face in both his hands and he said, 'Happy New Year, Vi.' And he leaned in and kissed my lips." My tummy flutters remembering that kiss. "His lips were soft and warm and so tender." My own wistful voice lingers. Helen sighs and I giggle before we both erupt into a fit of girlish laughter.

"My goodness." Helen pulls herself into a seated position. "Guess we'd better start on that English essay. Dinner will be soon."

I pull out my notebook and read the assignment notes. Helen lies on her stomach, propped up on her elbows, books spread on the bed.

"I'm really happy we met," I say.

She looks up from her books. "Who? You and John?"

"No, silly. You and me. I thank God for you every night. You are a good friend, Helen."

"Takes one to know one," she says with a wink.

✳ ✳ ✳

𝒩ovember 1940

WE GATHER at the church to celebrate Armistice Day. School is closed as we honor the soldiers who fought during the First World War. The unusually spring like weather adds to the celebration as the congregation files through the wide church doors to enjoy the warm air. Children run about, and women serve homebaked delights. I watch Iris laying out the apple pies she baked with Mother. I see, for the first time, a glimmer of maturity in her until she dashes off to join a game of hide-and-go-seek.

I pass by the men of the congregation and hear that, on this day of remembering all who died in battle, the men are deep in discussion about an impending stand against the war brewing in Europe. The irony escapes them, and I can't make sense of why our country is in this situation to begin with. I have always despised war. From everything I have learned in school or read in books, war is nothing more than a platform for humanity's evil. Even when John took me to see *Gone with the Wind* a few months back—though the movie was rich with the life and times of Scarlett O'Hara—the devastation of war remained at the forefront of my mind weeks later. I believe in standing up for others. I believe in protecting our homes, families, and friends. But the idea that going to war can solve problems goes round and round in my head. I have a hunch that war only ends up turning good, honest folk into people who do evil things, that the act of war makes them similar to the enemy they fight against.

"Hey, Vi. You look like you're stewing on something." John approaches where I sit on the front steps, a half chewed piece of straw hanging from the corner of his mouth.

"All this war talk is all." I shield my eyes from the sun.

"Today is Armistice Day, after all." John rounds the banister and sits on the step beside me. Our shoulders touch.

I shoot him a look that says, "I'm not an idiot," before my face softens. "Not that war. The new one everyone is so interested in."

"Britain is getting bombarded." He speaks like he might agree with the men I'd heard.

"Does that mean we should jump in and bring the war closer to home?" My anger surprises me. The words sound more infused than I had intended.

John chuckles at the heat rising in my cheeks. "No need to get all worked up. Is there anything you can do about the war anyway?" I stare at my hands, folded in my lap. "No. But—"

"But nothing, Vi. Don't waste your energy. Why don't we go for a walk, enjoy the day? Not many days like this left."

I shrug and agree to the walk, trying to let go of the nastiness of war.

We walk toward the pond, through a thick grove of trees behind the church. The time of year and lack of rain has shrunk the pond, leaving dry, cracked banks and putrid pond scum. We settle onto dry grass upwind from the pond and talk about school and the upcoming arrival of John's newest sibling. My family feels small compared to John's. The Smith house vibrates and bustles, and I am excited about a new baby to coddle and hold.

A wind sends a chill down my back. I remember the sweater I left laying across the end of my bed. John sees me shiver and wraps an arm around me while he looks to the sky. I lean into his embrace and watch the clouds sail past the blue backdrop. They are white and fluffy—happy clouds—but within minutes, the clouds darken, casting shadows on the ground, and the gusts of wind turn to an icy blast.

"We'd better head back," John says, examining the sky. "I don't like the look of this."

We walk hastily through the trees, our pace quickening with every creak and crack of limbs. My heart beats with an abandoned rhythm, and I place my hand over my chest. We step out of the dense foliage and onto the dirt path, nearly covered with snow already. I look up and snow cascades over my astonished face. The church is in sight, and we run to find our families and let them know we're safe.

Mother, Father, and Iris are waiting in Father's new Chevrolet, his first mode of transportation that does not require hay to run. The exhaust leaves the tailpipe in a plume of smoke. Father Smith is holding the door for Mrs. Smith as she lowers herself into the front seat of their four door Buick sedan. We all wave a quick goodbye before hurrying home, spurred on by the large snowflakes.

The ride home over slippery town roads has Mother bracing herself against the dashboard while Iris and I cling to each other in the back seat. Nobody speaks. Father's hands grip the steering wheel as the wind buffets the side panels, pushing the car about. The sky is dark, and the headlights barely illuminate the road. The snow is collecting faster than I have ever seen. The road is almost impossible to make out, and the snow banks grow by the minute.

Father turns onto the country road—the road is less slick, but the wind is more determined. We pass few cars, but Mother tells us to watch out for anyone who needs assistance. She bows her head and prays for anyone in the midst of this ferocious weather. The trip home from church usually takes fifteen minutes. We arrive at the farm an hour and a half later, shivering and covered in snow. Father parks the car as close to the back porch as possible. The phone is ringing as we dash into the kitchen, shaking the snow out of our hair. Mother lifts the phone to her ear as she motions for me to put water on to boil.

"Hello. Oh, Isabelle! Yes, we just got in. Terrible weather out there." Mother's voice is always louder when she is on the phone. "You managed all right? Good."

Isabelle is Isabelle Smith, John's mother. My shoulders relax, relieved the Smith family is safe, while I reach into the cupboard for mugs.

"I do hope this isn't how winter will be." Mother pauses. "Hello. Hello, Isabelle. Are you there?" Mother hangs up. "The line went dead. I guess the storm has taken down the phone lines."

Father stokes the fire as the four us huddle together, sipping tea and singing hymns. It storms all night, and in the morning, the car beside the back porch has all but vanished into a white snowdrift. The four of us take turns shoveling a path to the barn so we can water and feed the animals. Winter has arrived in South Dakota.

Weeks pass before we dig ourselves out from the snow drifts. When the roads are clear and safe, Father drives me back to Cedar Springs for school. I am relieved to learn that Helen has been stuck at her family farm at the opposite end of town. We arrive at the boarding house within a couple of days of each other, determined to catch up on our studies.

* * *

*S*eptember 1941

LITTLE EDWARD BOBS UP and down in John's arms, pure joy emanating from his doll like face. Mother Smith has left him in our care while she works in the kitchen, preparing for this evening's company. John and I have been back at school for a couple weeks, and his unwillingness to let go of his five-month-old baby brother is evidence that he misses being with Edward during the summer. I've come to view John in a new light these past few months. Though I've known he has a kind heart and a gentle smile, his patience and thoughtfulness shine through when he cares for Edward.

Not only can he instantly quieten Edward when he cries, he's in tune with Edward's needs, always anticipating. I wonder if he would be like this with our own children. I smile to myself, knowing he would.

John, Edward, and I are sitting under the shade of the porch, atop a blanket big enough for Edward to spread out on. The familiar Chevrolet, always with a fresh shine, pulls into the Smith driveway. I stand and wave as Father, Mother, and Iris step out of the car.

Iris races up the steps to wrap her arms around my waist. "I missed you," she says, giving me an extra squeeze.

"Iris, we've been apart six days." I rub her back to reassure her.

"That is one day more than usual."

"Yes, you are correct. I thought you'd enjoy a Saturday

evening dinner party. A good reason for me to have stayed in town this Friday." I try to keep the mood light, as I hope to sell her on the idea of me staying in town some weekends. Graduation is only nine months away, and I have begun to consider what I will do once school is finished.

"Oh, I do. Thank you for the invitation." Iris directs this comment to John. He stands and nods in reply.

John's sisters, hearing the commotion, come outside to pull Iris into their games.

Mother and Father join us on the porch, and we exchange greetings and hugs. John cradles Edward in the crook of one arm to shake Father's hand. Mother leans toward the baby and tickles his bare toes, which elicits a delighted squeal from Edward.

I gather the blanket from the porch, and we join the rest of the Smith family inside.

The evening is filled with laughter and good food. Once Edward is tucked in bed for the night, John's father pours his homemade wine. We retire to the front porch to enjoy the cool autumn breeze as we sip wine and listen to radio music filtering through the window. The evening feels magical. I capture the feeling in my heart, knowing the life I've dreamed of is in moments such as these.

✳ ✳ ✳

 ecember 1942

A YEAR HAS PASSED since the Japanese attacked Pearl Harbor. "America at war" is the only newsworthy topic these days, which is why I did not purchase a radio for my apartment in town. I would rather read, anyway, or spend evenings with John when his homework load is light.

I spend week days at the real estate office. I was awarded the front receptionist position a week after graduation, and I rented an apartment within walking distance of the office. Iris was crushed when she realized I would not return to the farm, the final blow to our tumultuous relationship. I chalk up our differences to the age gap and the fact that I had to grow up much faster than she. Even at thirteen, Iris tries to goad me into silly play or shenanigans every time I see her, testing my patience with each visit. I love her dearly, I do. But I believe the time has come for her to mature into a young lady and to leave all the silliness behind her.

We have fallen into a nice routine. I walk to church each Sunday and meet my family there. We sit through the service and gather for a shared meal afterward. So far, I have been able to enjoy my evenings with John, as well as the occasional dinner at the Smith house.

I will spend the holidays at the farm, since the office closes from the twenty-fourth until the first Monday of the new year. If the weather holds, John has promised to borrow his father's car to join my family for a festive dinner during the holiday season.

With my permanent move to town, John and I have enjoyed the luxury of daily time together. His chivalrous side shows each afternoon as he waits outside my office door to walk me home. I give him home cooked meals and fresh baked treats, and I once wondered if his dedication to escorting me home was because of the time with me or the food awaiting him at the end of the walk. Either way is compliment to me, my personality or my cooking.

***

*A*pril 1943

I CAN SMELL spring in the air. The crisp bite of winter is almost a memory, save for an occasional whippet of wind that seeks out any sliver of ivory skin beneath my nylon overcoat. As rain begins to fall, I clutch at my lapel, tuck my chin, and dash toward the awning across the street.

"Morning, Violet," calls Jim, the number one real estate agent in the office. I step inside and soak in the warmth from the radiator.

"Morning, Jim."

"Sold the Bower farm." He takes the damp coat from my arm and limps a little as he moves toward the picture window. He gives the coat a shake, releasing a cascade of tiny raindrops, and hangs the coat on the rack. "Could you finish up the paperwork today so I can drop the contract by this evening? Mrs. Bower said she'd bake me one of her blue ribbon cakes since I sold their farm real quick."

"Aren't you the favored one?" I tease, aware that Jim's interest lies with Mrs. Bower's daughter, Frances, more than with any cake.

"With rations and all," he stumbles, "I thought the gesture a kind one. You know, to thank me for the quick sale."

He runs his fingers through his hair with a boyish grin, and I am reminded how handsome he is. At thirty some years old, Jim has yet to marry. He lives above the real estate office and is entirely devoted to the business of property brokerage.

"I'd be happy to, Jim." I etch the mockery from my voice to convey my sincere intentions.

I set to work on the Bower paperwork as Jim retreats to his office, flushed but with regained composure.

The office is a hive of activity. Warmer weather begins the selling season. Nobody likes to move houses in the winter, so spring is lively. Those unable to keep up farms while their boys fight a war relocate to homes with more manageable expectations. Farms are being snapped up for a right good price, which keeps the office entrenched in the action. I enjoy the busyness—the work hours pass with ease. But on quieter days, I watch the town from the comfort of my desk chair. Men on their way to and from work, students headed to school, and mothers with baby carriages, collecting dry goods from the local mercantile. I am never bored. I am filled with my life's purpose and fulfilled by my employment. I have the luxury of independence and a little apartment a few blocks away. But my heart longs for the day I am a mother who pushes my own carriage, bakes my own bread, tends to my own vegetable garden, and welcomes my husband back into our home each evening. Those are my dreams, and John's, too, I imagine.

John and I have remained constant companions, best friends, two peas in a pod as his mother says. I finished school first, a year ahead. So while I work to save a little money for our future together, he is completing his final year of high school. A high school education is not common for young men, who often leave school to enter the work force. I am proud of John's dedication to his education and excited about his future opportunities as a businessman in our community. The war will be over by summer, I tell myself, and John and I will begin our life together.

*a*t four twenty on the dot, I see John striding toward the brick building. With patience a mile long, he tucks himself into the corner under the overhang and waits for me. My work day seldom ends early, so as I shuffle together the Bower documents and place them in the center of Jim's desk, John greets each passerby with a slight nod of his capped head.

As the clock ticks away the last few minutes, I tidy my desk and prepare to start fresh in the morning. The dark clouds have parted, and the sun follows a narrow escape route toward the horizon. The willowy rays warm the rain soaked street and make the asphalt shine like a fresh coat of paint. The office is quiet, except the steady tick of the radiator. Most of my coworkers leave much earlier in the day to meet with clients at their homes or places of work, brokering deals as they travel. Mrs. Boyd, the office manager, stays until five thirty. She insists she stays to work in peace, but I suspect home is a much lonelier place now that her son has shipped off to Europe to join the war effort.

"Good night, Mrs. Boyd. Have a fine evening." I peek through her office doorway.

"Thank you, Violet dear. Don't let that beau of yours wait any longer, now." She glances up from her accounting ledger. "I'll get the lights on my way out."

I remind myself to invite the Boyds to lunch next Sunday after church as I wrap my coat around my shoulders and loop my purse into the crook of my arm.

Outside, John's eyes sparkle in the disappearing sunlight as he wraps my free arm in his own. "Good evening, Miss Sanderson."

"John." I giggle like a schoolgirl at his formality. After so much time together, my tummy still flips whenever he smiles at me.

"I thought perhaps we could dine at the Fountain tonight." He cradles my elbow as we step into the street.

"Mmm, I'd enjoy a sweet tea right about now. Yes, that would be wonderful."

We stroll arm in arm toward our favorite diner, the warmth of the setting sun on our faces.

"How was your day?" John asks.

"Busy. Good, I mean. Busy is good. Lots to do with the start of the warmer weather," I say in a cheerful tone, though I know the day's intense concentration has tired me a little. "And you?"

"Same. The push is on to the end now. Prep for exams has begun." I nod and remember how my last semester of school felt like an eternity.

The Fountain is busy tonight, which is unexpected for a Tuesday. I suppose the little bit of sunshine brightened everyone's spirits enough to want an evening of social entertainment. We sit across from each other in a booth.

Within minutes, my sweet tea and John's chocolate shake arrive at the table. Sandwiches ordered, we sip our drinks as the restaurant's buzz fades to white noise.

I am lost in my thoughts when John reaches for my hand.

I seek solace in his gaze and realize this isn't the comfortable silence we usually share. This feels different. I am not familiar with this dead air.

John holds both my hands in his. I consider what to say, but no words fit this new, unknown silence.

"Vi, I've made a decision."

I watch him intensely and filter out the noise of the crowded diner. A proposal of marriage flits across my mind, but I know from the way he peers through me that this isn't one of those occasions. He leans closer and appears to beg for forgiveness before he has uttered a word. I know my heart is about to break. He clears his throat. "I've enlisted."

"What?" Astonishment mixes with a huge dose of confusion. "You've done what?" My instincts tell me to rip my hands from his, to run out of this diner and never look back. But my heart tells me there must be a misunderstanding. Why would I run away from the only person I've ever wanted to run toward?

"I understand you're upset." His eyes focus on the table. "I know I should have spoken with you about this, but I anticipated how difficult this would be, and I—I would have been drafted in a few months anyway." He looks straight into my angry blue eyes. "This is a stand I have to make, Vi."

I shake my head in bitter disagreement, wrenching my hands from his grasp. "You don't know that. The war may be over in six months. Why did you have to offer yourself up? How could they let you? You're not even nineteen yet. They aren't brazen enough to take boys off the schoolyard, are they?" My voice escalates into a high pitched shrill as fear engulfs me and my dreams for our future crumble.

Angry tears fueled by sheer panic sting my eyes. I dab them with a paper napkin and try to control my shaking voice. "Why wouldn't you talk to me first?" I hurl words full of fury. A moment of complete disdain engulfs me, and I want him to feel my fear.

"I knew you would talk your sense into me," he says in a hollow shadow of a voice.

"Of course I would have. We have plans. We have dreams. We were building a life together." My voice cracks as my love for this man bubbles out, broken. "I don't understand why you would throw our future away. Throw us away."

John drops his head into his hands, and when he searches my face again, his is stained with anguish. "You may never understand my reasons, but I did this for us. We can't live our dreams when others suffer. This is the only way I can ensure our happiness."

"I can guarantee you, John Smith, that I won't be happy when you're dead." I stand, eager to leave. I bump into the waitress who has approached our table and offer a weak apology as French fries scatter onto the floor. "I have to go."

✳ ✳ ✳

*D*ays drag on like months. My heart flutters more often than before. I decide my heart must be broken, and I have no idea how to cure its misery. I haven't seen John for three whole days. I suspect he's attempting to give me space, though sometimes I fear he has given up on me altogether, and I wonder what I'm doing. He chose this path. Surely, I should be the one who deserves to be angry. This thought causes tears to drop like spring rain, never ceasing once they start.

As the weekend nears, my anxiety grows. My emotions exhaust me as they alternate between anger and dread. At the office, I keep myself busy enough to get through each day. But today is Friday, and I've no idea how to pass two torturesome days before Monday. My apartment's walls close in a little more each evening, suffocating me as I lie awake reliving John's words as he called after me from the diner doorway. I consider telephoning Father and asking him to collect me for the weekend. I could most certainly use his warm, loving embrace, but the thought is overtaken by the admonishment I might receive when Mother hears how I behaved in public.

I am ashamed of how I acted, of how childishly I behaved. Until that night, I hadn't realized how much of a fantasy I had created about our dreamy future. I believed the fairytale with such vigor that I managed to block out life's realities. Perhaps John wasn't in the mindset of marriage at all. For all I knew, I might not be a good mother or wife. Perhaps this damned war will claim more than the love of my life. I may have to sacrifice all my dreams too. The more I consider potential outcomes, the more heartbroken I become, and I realize this isn't John's fault.

The responsibility belongs to me. I am guilty of my utopian dreams.

Mrs. Boyd stands at my desk, a worried frown running the width of her lips. "Violet dear, we should close up for the night."

"Oh! I hadn't realized the time. I am sorry. I hadn't meant to keep you late." I hastily gather papers into a pile.

"Oh no, dear. You aren't keeping me. John is ready for you. He has been outside for the past hour." Mrs. Boyd shuffles her stout frame sideways so I can see the door. "I didn't want him to wait any longer than need be."

"John?" I stand to gain a better view of the street. "I hadn't realized he was there." My cheeks warm. I bow my head to shield them from his intense eyes, gazing at me from outside.

"I am sure you two can sort through whatever the problem is." Mrs. Boyd pats my arm. "Oftentimes, one needs a little bump in the road to get their attention."

I nod without speaking, trying to keep my emotions in check.

She gives me a sly wink. "Off you go. Have fun." Mrs. Boyd waves to John through the glass and walks back to her desk.

I close the filing cabinet and wrap my coat around my shoulders before opening the door.

"Hello," I say. An unintended briskness fills my voice. "I apologize. I didn't realize you were out here."

"I wasn't sure you wanted to see me."

"Is that a question or a statement?" I ask.

"Vi, please. Can I walk you home? I'd like to talk with you."

Afraid of another public display if I speak, I loop my arm through his and tug him in the direction of my apartment.

* * *

$\mathcal{I}$ heat some soup and divide the broth between two bowls. I spread a thin layer of butter on two slices of bread before placing the plate on the table, a gourmet meal in my exhausted state.

I sit at the table, spoon in hand. "So. Talk."

John takes a drink of water and clears his throat. "I've been following the broadcasts. They need men, like me. Father says—"

"To do what? Sacrifice themselves so Uncle Sam can feel good about the war." I shake my head in disgust. "War is simply the government giving men permission to harm others. I don't want to believe you think killing is a tolerable pastime."

"I don't like the idea of killing any more than you do. But I do believe others are suffering needlessly. That is what I am standing up for."

"What about my suffering?" Tears flow down my cheeks. "Do you care about me? About my suffering?"

John slides his chair back from the table and swivels to face me.

Our knees touch, and his soft gaze is pleading. "I care more than you realize." His hand brushes the tears from my cheek. "I love you, Vi."

"Then don't go." My words are soft and desperate.

"I need to." He looks at his hands. "I promise you, I'll come back."

"You can't promise that, John." I pull my face away from his hand. "That's the point. I am afraid I will lose you forever."

"You don't think I am afraid, too? If I don't go and at least try to make a difference…" John pulls his chair closer to mine.

"Vi, I am more terrified of this war touching down on American soil than I am of dying. I can't let this war come home to you. I just can't." Tears rim the edges of his eyes. "I think about Edward. What world would he have to grow up in if the Germans controlled America?" He shakes his head with angry force. "I won't stand by and watch that happen. I won't."

We are at an impasse—John determined to fight, me determined to hold on to him with everything I have. We finish our meager meal. Spoons scrape the bottoms of our bowls. My body aches with exhaustion. The stress has taken a toll on me. I am desperate to lie down and escape this nightmare. I consider sending John away, but my brain and heart argue, leaving me in the middle of a river with two currents pulling in opposite directions. On one hand, I am desperate to be angry with him, to hurt him as he's hurt me. On the other, I want to take him in my arms and hold him for as long as I possibly can. Anything to ward off his inevitable departure.

* * *

*T*wo days later, I have not conceded my displeasure, yet I am seated beside John in the Smith family living room, offering support as he breaks the news—along with his mother's heart. My tears spring a leak as the reality of the situation moves across Mother Smith's face.

She gasps, "John—"

John's father interrupts, patting her shoulder. "We are very proud of you, son."

"But Samuel." His mother bursts into tears and turns her face into her husband's chest.

We all sit uncomfortably while Mother Smith heaves with grief.

As night falls, John and I take our leave and he walks me home.

The moment we step onto the front porch, John lets out a lungful of air. He pushes the hair back from his forehead. "Thank you for coming with me. I know you weren't keen to."

"You're welcome." I am already walking toward the front gate. "Breaks my heart to see her like that is all."

"She'll be all right. She'll have you to help her through. Won't she?" he says sheepishly.

"I'd do whatever I can for your mother. You know that, John."

"I guess I'm asking if you'll be there. Will you be there for me?"

"To be honest…I don't know about that. Not yet, anyway. I am still angry with you for not discussing this with me. I need some time is all." I shrug and turn toward home.

John chases after me. "I will give you time, Vi. I will write to you every day, as long as I can. Give me a chance to make it up to you. Please." He walks beside me, almost tripping on his sideways steps.

I can't help but giggle.

He wraps his arm around my waist and whispers in my ear. "I love you, Vi. I really do. Someday, I'm gonna marry you, just you wait and see."

A smile settles on my lips, and I pray he can live up to his promise.

*** *** ***

$\mathcal{T}$he day I have been dreading has arrived. John is scheduled to board the train this morning. His first destination is Fort Snelling, Minnesota. After that, he will be transferred to a camp for basic training— I presume before he is sent off to Europe. I have little information at this point, though I don't know if John is withholding details or if this is simply how the army operates during a war.

The scene at the station is emotional. John's mother clings to his arm with one hand and to her handkerchief with the other. His father, a foot shorter than John, appears to stand almost as tall as his son. His stiff posture must be an effort to keep his emotions intact. Apprehension fills the air as we stand like spooked creatures in the early dawn, aware of the thick undercurrent of trepidation.

Edward tugs at his brother's pant leg, with his thumb nestled between his closed lips. John stoops to pick him up and whispers into Edward's tiny ear. "Be a good boy for Mother, now."

The child nods and cradles his head in the crook of John's neck. My emotions rise into my throat, and I dissolve into a pile of sobs. I turn my head, trying to control my tears, and peer down the track. Smoke from the approaching train billows into the cool air. John will be gone in minutes.

John's sisters weep silently as they gather around their mother. As he addresses each of them, the first sign of emotion leaves his eye as a solitary tear. I realize his decision to enlist is not without personal pain, so I put aside my anger, still burning deep in my stomach, and prepare to bid him farewell.

As the train squeals to a stop, John takes my hand and pulls me away from his family. He wraps me in a tight embrace and kisses the top of my head before he murmurs into my ear, "Vi, wait for me. Will you? I promise. I will come back. I will."

"Mmhm," I manage between gulps of air.

He lets go too soon. I am desperate to hold on to the feeling of his arms around me. The smell of his skin. The sound of his words. I watch through tearblurred eyes as John picks up his bag and shakes his father's hand. He touches his mother's cheek with his palm and once more tousles the blond head of the littlest Smith. He lifts himself into the belly of the train without hesitation or a glance behind him.

John is a strong man, and he becomes stronger before my eyes as he heads into a war, leaving everyone he loves in spite of his own fears, determined to fight for the freedom of others. My heart's butterflies take flight as the train chugs out of the station, and I force myself to believe that everything will be all right.

* * *

ugust 20, 1943

THE SUMMER HEAT smolders off the brick building. Fans push stale air around the office. The women complain about their liquid lipstick while the men complain about having to wear suit jackets when they meet with clients. Steam rises a few inches from the street's dark surface, and the fountain shop down the road sells ice cream faster than they can make it. This is August in South Dakota, and this year's temperatures are higher than normal.

As four thirty rolls around, I see Father park the Chevy in front of the office. I've been spending more weekends at the farm since John left four months ago. I am not exactly avoiding the Smith family. I always visit with them at church on Sunday mornings, but I still have not determined whether our conversations are out of obligation or desire. So far, I have avoided Mother Smith's questions about John's letters, the ones I have yet to open. They arrive, almost daily, in my apartment building mailbox. I take comfort in knowing that he is well enough to write, though my inability to read them seems attached to the fear and anger filling up my body. So the letters sit, bundled in twine on my faded blue dresser—close enough to see every day, yet tied tightly enough that I resist the urge to read his thoughts, his feelings, his words.

Father steps out of the car and waves his big hand toward the large front window. Jim, the only brave soul left in the building with the heat climbing by the minute, enters the reception area and returns my father's wave.

"Mrs. Boyd left this for you before she headed home this

afternoon. I think you were on the phone." Jim hands me my paycheck.

"Thank you." I place the check in my purse as I stand to turn off the fans and flip the open sign to closed.

"Big plans for the weekend?" Jim stuffs his hands into his pants pockets as he rocks back and forth on his good leg.

"Not really." I shrug. "At the farm is all. I'm sure the garden will need tending to with all this heat."

"Sure has been some kind of weather. I never thought I'd be looking forward to rain." He laughs. "Well, have yourself a great weekend, Violet. I will see you on Monday." Jim waves once more to Father before disappearing toward his tiny office in the back of the building.

"Hello, darlin'," Father says as I close the office door behind me, overnight bag draped across my arm.

"Hi, Daddy." I embrace him before walking around to the passenger side.

We drive with the windows down. My hair whips about my face, but I make no effort to restrain the waves. Father talks about the week at the farm and Iris's success with the garden, though he warns she is eager for some help this weekend. I nod, understanding she has been talking nonstop about her plans for the weekend and that they clearly involve me. We pass the fields that lie between our farm and what was once the Smith farm, and I smile to myself when I see the big oak tree. I squint my eyes, blurring the view in an attempt to see John there, as I often found him—sitting among the tall grass under that tree, whittling a piece of a fallen branch, lost in his own thoughts. That is how I prefer to think of him. The boy who could do no wrong, until he did, of course. I know I am being childish, with a good measure of stubbornness to boot. Even so, I can't seem to get past these feelings, and with the war still raging, I'm not in any particular rush to do so.

*** *** ***

Sunday morning arrives sooner than I anticipate. Weekends at the farm are seldom dull. There are horses to exercise, pigs to water, and a garden that's wilting fast in the intense heat.

"Violet, I've had a thought." Mother watches me out of the corner of her eye. She stands beside me, slicing peaches for the oatmeal simmering on the stove.

"Yes?" I scoop the cut fruit into a bowl.

"I know being alone can be difficult at times such as these." She wipes her hands on her apron. "I thought perhaps you might join one of the volunteer war efforts in town. You know, to help pass the time."

I offer a weak smile. "I'm not sure I have the energy for that right now. I've found myself so tired these days."

"Of course, that could be this crazy heat." She waves her hand as if she could change the weather. "Perhaps, though, if you got involved, you might not feel so alone."

"Perhaps," I say, trying to neither commit nor dismiss. "I've not really felt alone, though. To be honest, I am angry with John for enlisting."

Mother's eyebrows rise as her head swivels to face me. "Angry? Really?"

"I know it sounds silly, but—"

"You're right. It does sound silly." Mother turns her attention back to the peaches. "You can't control others' actions, Violet. You can only control your reaction to them."

I shrug, knowing when to cut my losses in a conversation with Mother.

"Mrs. Beattie from church is quite involved in the

organization of the girls' volunteer efforts. I will put in a mention for you."

Mother's intentions are clear. I will soon meet with Mrs. Beattie, whether I want to or not.

Sunday mornings are filled with song, worship, family, and fried chicken. After I moved to town for school, my family met each week at church. Iris, never shy, nudged anyone aside so she could sit with me. Her favored position was to hold my hand during sermon. Not much has changed in that regard. Iris steps over Father's toes to slide in beside me.

"Mother says I can sleep over with you next Saturday if you aren't coming to the farm. I can meet them at church on Sunday."

"Mother says, does she?" I wonder what possessed Mother to offer such an invitation, and without checking with me first. Irritation at the thought of Iris's extended company smolders. At fourteen, Iris has yet to embrace the qualities of a young woman. Her exuberance for life, though refreshing, can test my patience on even a good day. "She says we can even go to a picture show and have popcorn and soda." Iris bulldozes her way through conversations like she does everything else in life. "After that, we can go to the mercantile and pick out some fancy candy."

"We'll have to see." I hadn't intended for the edge in my voice to sound so cross. I smile, trying to dampen the fire burning in her belly. Reverend Campbell takes his place at the pulpit, and I shush her into conformity.

The sermon is lovely, with three of my favorite hymns. During prayer, Reverend Campbell mentions each man from our congregation who's serving our country, including John. I put aside my anger and bow my head, adding an extra prayer for his safe return.

We gather outside the steps with white treads peeling in the summer sun. Mother Smith wraps me in a warm hug as my parents shake hands with the reverend. Father Smith waits patiently for his turn before he puts his arm around my shoulder, giving me a squeeze.

Iris chatters nonstop to Mother, telling her I've said yes to a sleepover next weekend.

"Iris." My voice is serious. "I said we'll have to see. Someone would need to bring you to town on Saturday, and you can't always presume Father will have the time or the desire to do so."

"She's been asking for months," Mother says flatly as she exchanges a hug with John's mother. Iris's consistent pestering eventually elicits a weary surrender from anyone she harasses. From the look on Mother's face, I can tell she has reached her limit.

"If she wouldn't be too much of a bother, honey." Father lowers his voice and leans toward me so Iris won't hear. "I can make both trips to town next week. It'll give me a chance to check on that dripping kitchen faucet you mentioned, too. I know an overnight with you would mean a lot to your sister, and to be honest, I suspect Mother can't take much more talk on the subject."

I understand that "no" is not an option. "All right. You can have a sleepover, but I'm not promising any fancy candy."

Iris jumps in the air, her dress billowing as her feet hit the ground. "I knew this would work out. I just knew it."

I can't help but smile at her enthusiasm as Iris bursts out her news to John's sisters.

We pick a flat piece of shady grass and lay out our blankets. Since the Smith family moved to Cedar Springs, where John's father works in the bakery, Sundays are the only day our parents visit. I only realized after John left for basic training just how connected our two families are. Prior to their move into town, our farms were close enough to pass by. There were occasional shared buggy rides to school and extra helping hands whenever one was in need.

We empty baskets filled with coleslaw, potato salad, and fried chicken onto the blankets. Mother has baked a wild plum pie, and my mouth waters as the scent reaches me.

The younger kids run about, playing tag and other games while the adults relax in the shade. I adore these moments, surrounded by those I love, but John is never far from my thoughts. My heart aches as I yearn for him, so far away.

*** * * ***

I am far from surprised when Mrs. Beattie's tall, lanky frame stands before me at the office the following Tuesday. She offers a thin smile as she peers across her narrow, pointed nose, sizing me up. She goes through a list of tasks I might be suited for, rattling them out as if I should understand what they mean. I agree to attend the information session the following evening, and after a quick hello to Mrs. Boyd, she is off to sweet talk another unsuspecting young woman.

"So wonderful of you to join the effort, Violet." Mrs. Boyd stands on her tiptoes to reach the top file drawer.

"I am not certain I have the time. Or the energy. Or the desire, for that matter. But Mother feels I should become involved. She is worried I am too lonesome."

"Of course you are, dear. All those left behind feel a bit blue." She says this so matter of factly that I am struck by the realization that I have begun to wallow in self pity.

"Of course. I am sure the meeting will be well worth my time."

She cocks her head to one side as she appraises the skepticism in my voice. "Yes, dear. I can promise you that."

Mrs. Boyd pivots to leave, but pauses in front of my desk. "I know the situation is not easy, war and all. God knows I understand what you are going through. The worry, the grief, the sense of doom over your head." She gently places her plump hand on my arm. "I'd be happy to join you for the information meeting if you'd like. I can introduce you to some of the other girls."

I recognize an olive branch from a kind woman. "That would

be nice. Thank you, Mrs. Boyd. I appreciate the gesture and your time."

The temperature rises as the day passes, and flies circle in a waft of stale air. My thoughts revolve around the meeting at the Red Cross. I hate that I was goaded into it, but I know better than to ignore Mother's advice. I wonder, for the first time, if John would want me to join the war effort. Then I think I don't care much about what John would want. By the time four thirty comes around, I have argued myself to death. I am sick of the anger within me. Mrs. Boyd's comment made me recognize the guilt that lies there, too. Juggling these emotions is a fulltime job. I have a small desire to move past them, but I can't seem to let John off the hook. So I hang on.

Wednesday evening, Mrs. Boyd and I assemble with twenty other nervous young women. The meeting is in an empty commercial building a few blocks from our office. The large red letters of the American Red Cross are painted over the previous tenant's white washed business name. Rows of chairs face a long table, where two women sit flanked by stacks of papers. Mrs. Boyd introduces me to the ladies at the table, and they give me a pencil and a package of papers to review, fill in, and hand back to them at the end of the meeting.

Mrs. Boyd chats with women near the coffee station while I sit near the back of the room to review my information package. I fill in my name and address, and I fabricate a reason for my interest in the volunteer program. I scan the documents, glancing over the many opportunities within the organization. Administrative Corps catches my eye, since I am already trained for that type of position. But I continue to read, hoping to find a task a little less like my day job and a little more inspirational than paperwork.

As I flip the page, I catch a flash of red hair from the corner of my eye. "Helen?" I ask as the tall, lanky girl pivots toward me, a smile erupting across her face.

"Oh my gosh! Violet. Wow." She sits beside me, and we wrap our arms around each other. "I can't believe you're here." Helen cocks her head to one side. "Why are you here? Does that mean John—" Her hand flies up to cover her open mouth. "I'm so sorry." She wraps me in another hug and tears sting my eyes.

Helen pulls away, wiping her own damp cheeks. "Me, too. Robert was drafted seven months ago."

"I'm sorry, Helen. I don't think I know Robert."

"No, he's a few years older. We met in July, just after graduation." She examines her hands, clasped together in her lap. "We were to be married in September."

"I can't believe we haven't seen each other." I rub her shoulder, only now missing the companionship we shared in school.

"Well, you stayed in town to work, and I went back to the farm until I could save enough money for college."

"That's right. You wanted to be a nurse. How is that going?" I ask, eager to change the subject from her indefinitely postponed wedding.

"I never went." Helen sighs. "I fell in love instead. Robert was going to be a good provider, and he wanted to start a family straight away, so I put it off. Foolish now, I guess. I don't have Robert or a career."

"No, not foolish Helen. There is nothing foolish about falling in love." I shake off the notion that my words are good advice for more than just Helen.

"So, what volunteer group are you joining?" Helen brushes her hair back with long, pale fingers.

"I've only started to read through all this." I hold up the papers. "I'm only here because Mother insisted."

Ignoring the displeasure in my voice, Helen says, "I've decided to join the Production Corps."

"What is the Production Corps?"

"Sewing for the most part, at this chapter's location. But I've read how great of an impact the comfort kits and the surgical bandages have on the health and welfare of the troops. I knew straight away that if, God forbid, Robert needed surgery," Helen says raising her eyes to heaven, "I wanted to do everything in my power to be part of the movement that brings our fellas home."

"Production Corps. Okay, I'll join you. Though I haven't sewn before." I laugh. "I will give it a try. This could be interesting and, at the very least, entertaining."

Helen laughs and squeezes my hand. "I look forward to spending more time with you, Violet."

"Me, too," I say, and I really mean it.

I don't need to read any further. My decision is firm, so I close the booklet and wait for the meeting to begin. Mrs. Boyd sits beside me, coffee in one hand, homemade cookie in the other. I introduce her to Helen.

"You all settled?" she asks, nibbling at the edge of her treat.

"I am, I suppose. I want to make those comfort kits. I'm not much of a sewer, but I am eager to learn."

"Wonderful, Violet. This is wonderful news." She jostles me with her shoulder. A drop of coffee dribbles down the side of her cup, but she doesn't notice. She shines at me like a proud mother goose.

The meeting begins, and as I listen to the importance of the volunteer effort, I suddenly wish I had even more time to offer, more to give. I suppose Mother knew what she was talking about, though I have no intention of admitting that to her.

I feel a renewed sense of ambition, a sensation I haven't felt since John delivered the wretched news of his enlistment. The ambition lifts me up, if only for a moment, from the despair that has engulfed me these past months. Perhaps, in this place, I may work out my anger with John, though I'm not certain he deserves a pass just yet.

The women describe each volunteer position, and hands go up as young women sign up. I learn that the Productions Corps is the largest of the Red Cross's volunteer movement and has been instrumental in supplying dressings for surgical wards, which are dispensed to hospitals around the country and beyond.

A small group of four, which includes Helen and myself, has volunteered for the Production Corps. We huddle together while the leader of the local chapter's Production Corp details our next steps.

"We meet every Monday, Wednesday, and Thursday." She points to a doorway that leads to the back of the building. "On the other side of that door is the room where we sew. You are, of course, welcome to use any free day to work on projects, but we do require you to be as committed as possible. Our troops need all the support we can give them, after all."

We adjourn our meeting, promising to be present the next evening for an "introduction to sewing" class. I'm relieved such a class exists. I locate Mrs. Boyd and say goodbye to Helen, already anticipating seeing her again tomorrow evening. I walk Mrs. Boyd home and thank her for her company, before walking the additional five blocks to my own apartment, eager to make a quick sandwich and turn in for the night.

I step a little lighter on my way home. For the first time in months, I feel comfortable in my own skin. I scold myself for my moody behavior and decide that, to move forward, I must stop glancing back. The road I must travel is before me, and I am thankful to have found a purpose amidst this war.

I crawl into bed, wearing my lightest cotton nightgown. I tilt my head toward the open window and watch the curtain billow in the light breeze. I enjoy the feel of the wind as the soft air caresses my cheek. I drift to sleep with images of John, and my hardened shell of anger begins to crack, if only a sliver.

✳ ✳ ✳

*D*ecember 1943

THE WINTER WIND bites my face as I tuck my chin into my jacket's upturned collar. My scarf, no match for today's frosty temperature, trails behind me like a flag whipped about by wind. These past few icy days have caught me by surprise, as the weather has been unseasonably warm until now. The air feels as if winter realized its mistake and is determined to make up for those early days.

I walk with urgency as the clouds gather, threatening snow. The wind slams the door behind me as I enter the Red Cross volunteer building. My cheeks sting in response to the warm air as I peel off my mittens and hat.

"Violet." Mrs. Boyd bustles over to greet me at the door. "Oh dear. Sure is a blustery one out there."

"Yes, indeed." I shake my jacket from my shoulders before managing to extract myself from the scarf threatening to strangle me.

"Not to worry, dear. Not to worry. A cup of hot cocoa and you'll be good as new. This weather is not fit for man nor beast."

"Thank you, Mrs. Boyd. That is most kind of you." My toes tingle as sensation returns to them.

"Nonsense, dear. Only take a minute. No trouble at all. Now come, let's get you a warm drink." She leads me to the coffee station, her short, thick legs moving with a speed that contradicts their size.

Lauren and Beth are in the sewing room. I hang my coat on

the rack, my wayward scarf tucked into an armhole. I sip from my mug, and the steam rises to meet my nose.

"We figured you'd thought better of sewing tonight." Lauren glances up from her fabric to cast me a mischievous smile. "Thought perhaps the weather was too much for you to venture out."

"I'm not late." I blow on my cocoa. "Early for tomorrow is all." I send her a playful wink.

"Don't mind her." Beth stands with both hands on her hips, her role as a schoolteacher evident in her posture. She covers her laughter with a thin veil of seriousness. "She only arrived herself, she did. Hustled her butt into that chair an instant before you walked in."

Lauren throws a rolled eye look in Beth's direction before she laughs and pats the seat beside her. The four of us—Lauren, Beth, Helen, and I—have become fast friends.

"Where's Helen?" I ask. "Sure isn't like her to be late." None of us, in fact, have ever beaten Helen to the sewing room. Each of us has tried to arrive early and beat her here, to no avail. Helen always arrives first. Until today that is.

Beth shrugs as she settles herself in front of her machine. She examines the thread and begins to pump the pedal.

The machines hum, and our voices climb over the sound as Lauren tells an animated story about a humorous mishap at the hardware store, the family business where she works. Beth and I join in the laughter when Lauren, talking with her hands, forgets to remove her foot from the pedal, which results in an out of control sewing machine.

Lauren squeals, fueling our laughter even further until Mrs. Beattie enters the room.

"Sorry, ma'am," Beth says at the sight of the prim, nononsense woman.

"What? No. Beth," she stammers with an apologetic smile.

"Ma'am?" Lauren says as Mrs. Beattie stands in the doorway with a strained expression.

"Ladies," she says, "I have some unfortunate news."

We wait. All three of us hold our breath as Mrs. Beattie finds her words.

"Helen won't be with us for a while. She has suffered a great loss." Beth gasps, bows her head and motions the sign of the cross over her body.

Mrs. Beattie begins again. "Helen's beau, Robert, fell from a ladder a few weeks back. He broke several bones in his leg. The leg became infected and was amputated."

"Oh, dear God," Lauren whispers. Her nail bitten hand covers her mouth. "Poor Robert. Poor Helen."

Mrs. Beattie's throat emits a strangled sound. "The infection spread. Robert passed away yesterday. News reached his mother this afternoon."

"Died?" My voice wavers as the news hangs in the air. "How does one go from a fall off a ladder to dead in a few weeks?"

Beth stands and positions herself behind me. She hugs my shoulders as Lauren leans in to both of us. We sit huddled together in a weak effort to support one another. We mourn for our friend and her Robert.

Mrs. Beattie excuses herself, apologizing again for the interruption and the news.

After several minutes of silence, I follow Lauren and Beth's lead and stand behind a sewing machine. The sewing is slow and methodical. The machines drum out a beat, and the white noise traps me in my own thoughts. I try to hold the panic at bay, but fear creeps in. My thoughts are with John. How many ladders does he climb? I have been under a delusion of his safety as his letters pile up on my dresser, thinking only of wartime injuries, not those resulting from mundane tasks. I have taken solace in Mother Smith's assurance that he is still immersed in training. I have convinced myself that he is distant from real danger.

My eyes dart around, and an intense pressure pushes against my chest. Breathing becomes unbearable. The room feels smaller, thick with warm, stale air. With my eyes elsewhere, I leave a trail of crooked stitches on the fabric. My heart pounds, surely loud enough for others to hear. My imagination is ignited with possibilities. What if he is in an automobile accident or a target practice mishap? What if he cuts himself peeling potatoes and gets an infection? Here I've been worried about tanks, guns, and Germans when I should have seen fit to worry about ladders.

I bolt upright, my chair tipping backward to the floor. "I have to go," I stammer, hands shaking at my sides. "I have to go now." I walk with haste toward my jacket hanging on the hook near the door. I push my arm into the sleeve but it's obstructed. "Damned scarf," I mutter as I wrench the long, thick fabric from the sleeve, discarding it to the floor.

"Violet? Are you all right?"

I hear Beth's voice as she stands to face me, but her words don't penetrate my brain. Frustrated with my coat, I toss the heavy wool over my arm, grab my purse, and run out of the building. The door slams behind me as my face embraces the cold. I gulp in welcomed air, before my body betrays me and gives way to a shiver running the length of my spine. My cheeks sting as the frigid wind turns my tears into crystals. My shoes, unsuitable for the weather, slide over the snow dusted street as I stride with drunken steps toward home. Toward the comfort of my cozy apartment. Toward the words in John's letters.

The tragic news of Robert's death ignites a desire to know more. To feel more. To be more for both myself and for John. I've been childish to hold on to this anger. I turn left and see the lights of my building, flickering in the distance. I dash toward the comfort of my apartment with little regard for my appearance as desperation propels me foreword. Chills fill my body, but I realize the frigid night air is not the cause of my shivers. The reality of war is at fault.

I throw open the door to the apartment lobby, gasping for breath. I pause before the narrow mailboxes. The flutter has erupted in my chest. I ignore the feeling and pull open the mailbox labeled 2B, retrieving the single envelope covered with John's neat handwriting. Without a moment's thought, I draw the envelope to my nose and inhale deeply. I climb the stairs to my apartment, knowing I want John in my life. War or no war, my heart still beats for him, and the time has come to tell him so.

I throw my coat and purse on the bed and fetch the letters bound with twine. Seven months of almost daily correspondence. I grip the latest envelope between my teeth as I balance the pile, walking through the kitchen toward the dining area. The envelopes land with a thump onto my tiny eating table. I stifle a yawn. I've little time to be tired. I must read John's words before I can write back. I don't have a clue what I will say. All I know is that I won't be able to live with myself if the last words John hears from me were fueled by resentment, anger, and self pity. I sit in front of the pile and retrieve the first letter from its imprisonment.

MONDAY, May 3, 1943

Dearest Violet,

Only a week has passed since I watched your sad face vanish from sight. I don't think you could see me pushing my cheek against the window, but I never took my eyes off you while the train pulled out of the station. My heart is heavy, knowing how unhappy you are about my decision. I never meant to cause you pain. I've only ever wanted to love you and for you to love me. I do hope you will forgive me in time. Mother says that time heals all wounds. I pray she is right. I am counting on it, to tell you the truth.

You are in my heart and on my mind always. Love,

John

. . .

I LAY THE LETTER FACEDOWN, tucked into the envelope. I imagine him here in front of me, our knees touching. I can see his eyes pleading with me. I wish I could go back in time. I sigh and tear open the next envelope. I read several more letters before I pause to sip my now lukewarm tea.

TUESDAY, May 11, 1943

Dearest Violet,

I have arrived at basic training. The place is a hive of activity, men running this way and that. They always seem to be in some sort of a hurry. I'm sure I will get used to the busyness, but for now, the place feels like a thriving city, nothing like the snail's pace of Cedar Springs. I settled in to my bunk fine, and I have met a few guys about my age. Boys from all over have traveled here to fight this war. I enjoy hearing stories of life in places like San Francisco and the backwoods of Montana. Places we should visit once this war is over.

Tomorrow, the real work begins. I look forward to the training. Idle hands and all. I hope my letters are reaching you. I've sent a couple to Mother and Father, too, though no replies have come my way yet. I am eager for word from you, Vi. Please let me know that you are well.

You are in my heart and on my mind always. Love,

John

GUILT BUBBLES within me as I drop the letter onto the pile. These letters, from months ago, requesting correspondence from me are heavier than the paper they are written on. What kind of man holds on that long with no reciprocation? I've been foolish to let my anger control my actions. I've never been more ashamed of myself than I am in this moment. I am desperate to write to him, to say that I am still his.

Sunday, June 27, 1943

    Dearest Violet,

    I hope this letter finds you well and that you are enjoying summer weather. The days are long and hot here, and the nights seem shorter than they ought to be. You were in my dreams last night, so my sleep was fitful as I tried to grasp hold of you. Your smile draws me in, but those crystal blue eyes of yours make me believe you are real. Time is passing quickly, a good situation, I think, since I don't much enjoy digging foxholes in the clay. Though I know they may one day save my life, I hope that European soil is a might bit softer.

    Every day is training day here. We rise early. March everywhere. Test our skills and learn new ones along the way. Crawling through mud under barbed wire is by far my least favorite, but a necessary task, I suppose. Not much time for thinking is left at the end of the day, once I've washed my uniform and crawled into bed. By design, I imagine. Nobody wants soldiers with fresh weapons training to have too much time to think of where they'd rather be.

    I apologize that my letters are short. Time is short, as well. But I sure could use a few words from you. If you could spare me a few thoughts, I'd appreciate the gesture.

    You are in my heart, in my dreams, and on my mind always.
Love,

    John

My heart feels as if it is free falling to the pit of my stomach. I am only a fraction of the way through the first bundle of envelopes, each one a glimpse into his daily life. Each letter reassures me of his continued love for me. I'm certain Mother Smith has written to him, letting him know I am well, but I wonder if he has told her about my lack of correspondence. Another wave of regret washes over me. Until now, I had thought anger would eat me up inside. I'm beginning to realize that shame may be just as powerful. I've got to fix this at once.

I reach for the letter that arrived today and slice open the envelope with brash urgency.

FRIDAY, December 3, 1943

Dearest Violet,

Winter has reached us here at camp. The tents, which seemed airless and intense this past summer, are now unable to keep a light breeze at bay. I've taken to wearing the mittens Mother

knitted me to bed each night, sliding them on under the shield of darkness so as not to alarm the other men. The new fallen snow has inspired a variety of maneuvers, which exhaust us even further. Some days I dream of digging foxholes again. Same as that stubborn old wandering bull at home who couldn't stay put, the grass is always greener on the other side of the fence.

Mother sent me a fine photograph of the family last week. Edward is growing faster than I imagined. Her letters seem all right. I don't imagine her worry is less, but she is keeping solid footing. I'm not sure what to think about the holidays. The thought of Mother's bread pudding makes my mouth water. I don't imagine there will be much celebration here, but I'll be attending a service on base the twenty-fourth. I will be thinking of you, especially that evening, Vi. Praying that you will find it in your heart to forgive me. I miss you every day.

You are in my heart and on my mind always. Love,

John

. . .

"I'VE GOT to set things right," I say to myself as I step into the kitchen and pull open the drawer for stationary and pens. I return to the table, pushing aside the half empty cup of cold tea.

THURSDAY, December 9, 1943

Dear John,

I hope this letter finds you healthy and well. The weather has changed to a bitter cold, which is a far cry from only a few days ago, when we still had somewhat balmy temperatures. Balmy for December, anyway.

I'm not certain of what to say. I owe you an apology for my lack of correspondence. I have been so angry with you for leaving. So angry that I let my righteousness cloud my feelings for you. This may sound delusional, but somehow the anger made me feel strong. I guess I was frightened that if I let my guard down, I would crumble without you here. That is not fair to you. I realize that now. I am truly sorry. Please forgive me.

Tonight was the first time that I read your letters. I know, I know. Insane as this may sound, I allowed your letters to pile up. They reminded me that you were well and, in some way, also fueled my anger. Today was different, though. I received news that unsettled me to my core, and to be honest, I am not yet sure how to deal with the fallout. You remember Helen? My roommate from the boarding house. Helen and I have been spending quite a bit of time together at the Red Cross since I began volunteering there. Actually, Mother insisted I join, but that is a story for another time. Helen joined at the same time. Her beau, Robert, was drafted. They were to be married this past September. The news is dreadful, John. Robert fell from a ladder, breaking several bones. While in the hospital, he contracted an infection, and a few weeks later he died. Robert's mother and Helen only received word today. He was in the navy, already stationed in Europe.

John, I was overcome with grief. My heart aches for Helen, and I fear there is no way to comfort her in this time of devastation. I feel so helpless and small. I began to worry for you, and I prayed you weren't scheduled to climb any ladders. I know this sounds silly, given that you are at war and all, but I hadn't considered such tasks could take soldiers' lives.

I think of you every day, all day to be precise, and pray you will be safe and well and that this war will end so you can return to me. Please be safe and know that you are loved.

All my love, Violet

As soon as I put down the pen, tears erupt from my eyes and roll down my cheeks. They spill onto the letter. Large droplets blur the ink. In this moment, with my heart in pieces, I understand that even if John returns unharmed, I may not survive this war. Now, more than ever, I want to escape to the quiet life I had envisioned for us. A little house, a vegetable garden, children running about the yard, and John coming home to us each evening, happy and well. A thousand years seem to have passed since we were last happy. With no end in sight, a thousand more years could pass before our dream becomes reality, and even that is uncertain, with so many obstacles in our way.

I leave the letter to dry on the table until morning, when I will place the pages in an envelope and then in the postal box. I stumble into the bedroom, leaning on walls for support. With no energy left in my tired and tortured body, I crawl under the covers, fully clothed, and cry myself to sleep.

* * *

The next few days move like molasses in winter. Helen refuses to see anyone and has sequestered herself in Robert's old bedroom. The first Saturday after the news of his death, Lauren, Beth, and I try to convince her to let us in. We want to sit with her, be there for her. The only sound from inside the room is her feet shuffling away from the door. The bed creaks and we presume she has lain back down. In the Palmers' front room, we attempt to make small talk with a woman who, only a few days ago, lost her only son. After a painful hour of waiting for Helen to emerge, spent in virtual silence, we take our leave and promise to return when Helen is ready for company. Mrs. Palmer thanks us for our condolences and our patience. She dabs her eyes with a handkerchief, the initials RP embroidered on the corner.

The walk back to town is quiet. None of us know what to say. The world feels as if it's shifted and is no longer seated in place. We have been changed. The war has forced us to change. To become scared little women who put on brave faces while we pretend to save the world by sewing. This nonsense churns inside me and simmers like a volcano. I swallow hard and try to push down the thick, fiery emotions as the fumes threaten to bubble and spew.

We pass the movie theater, and I am drawn in by the colorful posters telling stories of love and happier times. The popcorn reaches my nostrils and my tummy rumbles. Joy has been vacant from my life for too many months. I long for a moment resembling normal. "Let's go to a movie."

"A movie?" Lauren and Beth say in unison, puzzlement casting shadows across their faces.

"Yes. A movie. We need to escape for a little while. We need to forget about this stupid war and pretend we are just three girls out on the town, out to enjoy a show and a little popcorn." I sound more confident and exuberant than I feel, but somewhere deep within me, I understand that the only way to survive this chaos is to find moments of sanity that remind us who we are and where we come from.

Together, we turn toward the theater, link arms, and stroll to the ticket booth with our heads held high. "Three, please, for *In Old Oklahoma*," I say. "My treat, ladies." I force a smile and walk with purpose toward the popcorn.

* * *

ecember 24, 1943

CHRISTMAS EVE FALLS ON A FRIDAY. The real estate office closes at noon and remains closed until the first week of 1944. I plan to spend the holidays with Mother, Father, and Iris before I return to town to visit John's family for a few days—a visit that is long overdue. When John's mother invited me, I knew it was time to mend a few fences. Father is to collect me from my apartment at one o'clock, so I hurry home through the fresh snow to pack the remainder of my possessions.

Before I climb the stairs to my second story apartment, I stop to check the mailbox, desperate for a letter from John. I close my eyes, squeeze them tight, and say a little prayer before I open the box.

"Thank you, God," I whisper to myself when I spot the single envelope leaned inside the narrow mail slot. I retrieve the envelope and clutch the letter to my breast. Overcome with gratitude, I begin to close the wooden door when I notice a package. The little box is half hidden by shadows. I reach inside for the small, square package wrapped in plain brown paper. The return address says "Private First Class, John Smith." *Private First Class*, I think. *Why, John has been promoted.* A thrill of excitement emits from me like a beacon, and I dash up the stairs two at a time, eager to tear open the package.

I drop my purse onto the kitchen table and reach for the scissors in the kitchen drawer. I gently slice the edges of the paper and extract the tiny box from the layer of wrap. Tucked inside the little box is a note. "For Violet. The song in my heart plays only for you. Merry Christmas. Love, John." Beneath the note is a silver charm bracelet with only one charm, a heart. I hold the charm at eye level and watch the light sparkle off the shiny bit of silver. A tear snakes down my face and ends at my lips. I taste the salt before the tear evaporates in the dry air.

I want desperately to close the bracelet's clasp around my wrist with my left hand, but Father will be here any minute. Even as the thought forms, there is a knock at my door.

"Daddy." I allow him to wrap me in his immense arms. I can smell horse hair and hay on his clothes. I breathe in the scent and allow the comfort of home to infiltrate my senses. I feel small and safe again.

"Hello, pumpkin. Good to see you. You need me to take your bag?"

"I'm so sorry. I'm almost ready. I'll grab the last few pieces." I tuck a strand of hair behind my right ear and touch my hand to my forehead, thinking of what my half packed suitcase is missing.

"What's this?" He fingers the shiny bit of silver still grasped in my palm.

"I've just opened the package. A gift from John. For Christmas." I hold the bracelet up for him to see.

"I'll be." Father angles his head to one side, for a better look at the heart shaped charm. "Mighty thoughtful young man, isn't he? Why don't we put that bracelet where it belongs." He fastens the clasp around my wrist with more ease and dexterity than I would have expected from his thick, calloused fingers. "That's better," he says.

I blush. "Thank you." I move hurriedly toward the bedroom to gather the rest of my things.

Father carries my suitcase while I juggle the presents I have wrapped and tied with ribbon, ready to give away in the morning. As we are about to walk out the door, I remember the unopened letter on the table and pluck the envelope from the discarded wrapping paper. I follow Father into the hall and lock my apartment door. My bracelet slides on my wrist, and I smile at the new reminder of John.

We arrive at the farm. Iris, still young in spirit, blasts down the porch steps. She runs full speed into my arms and almost knocks me to the frozen ground. I've no idea what keeps her feet planted on this earth. Her constant excitement is strong enough to bubble over and make her fly.

"Are those for me?" She nods her head at the presents loaded in my arms.

"Not all of them," I tease. "But perhaps there is one or two with your name."

This Christmas, despite the circumstances of war, I am eager to bestow the gifts I've brought for my family. I hope they enjoy them as much as I enjoyed making them. For weeks, I have worked with the sewing machine Tuesday evenings, when the Red Cross isn't using them for the war effort. With a little help from Mrs. Boyd, I managed to sew a new dress for Iris and a purse to match. I am certain they will make her feel all grown up when she wears them to church. For Mother, I have stitched two pillows, filled with fluff, for the living room sofa. Father was a challenge. After much consideration, I decided on a horse blanket embroidered with "Sanderson Equestrian Farm."

Iris takes my suitcase from Father and half carries, half drags my bag to the porch. Mother stands in the doorway, hair pulled back in a kerchief, arms crossed over her bosom. She watches Iris's attempt to be helpful, and though she doesn't say a word, she bites the corner of her bottom lip and I know she wants to correct her youngest daughter's actions. Mother embraces me with a quick hug before she ushers us in to the kitchen and hurries to close the door against the winter chill.

Roasting chicken spits and sizzles in the oven. The counter is covered with root vegetables ready to be washed and cooked. I peek into the living room to see the tree aglow in the corner. I carefully place the packages under the fragrant boughs and pause to touch one of my favorite ornaments. Memories of past Christmases flood my mind. Christmas has always been a happy time. Even when there wasn't much money, Christmas meant family games, stories read aloud, and the hope that comes so naturally during the season.

This is my first Christmas in five years without John. I feel my bracelet, hidden under the cuff of my woolen coat. I, at least, have the company of my family. My heart quivers when I envision him alone, without loved ones with whom to celebrate the holiday. When these occasional dark thoughts enter my consciousness, I imagine him shivering beneath a thin, itchy blanket—alone and exhausted. I push the thought from my mind and instead hope that the parcel of embroidered handkerchiefs and sweets arrived in time for him to enjoy. Without time to start from scratch, I purchased a set of twelve handkerchiefs from a shop in town. I spent every spare moment embroidering his initials into the corners, an idea inspired by Robert's mother. I sprayed each one with the scent of my favorite perfume before packaging them with sweets and milk chocolate for John to savor. I mailed the parcel over a week ago, in the hope that he might open my gift in time for Christmas.

I lift my bag from Iris's arms and deposit my suitcase onto my old child sized bed. "Won't a sleepover for Christmas be fun, Violet?" Iris bounces up and down on her own identical bed.

"Sure will be," I say with a trickle of frustration. How wonderful life must be for Iris, to be oblivious, unaffected by the war. I kick myself for such an insensitive thought. I smile at her youthful face and remind myself that all she should know is happiness. I wouldn't want her to live any other way.

While we scrub vegetables and set the Christmas Eve table, complete with pinecones and greenery, Mother and I talk about life in town, work, and the snow falling beyond the kitchen window. I feel her eyes as she steals glances at my bracelet. She made a fuss about the bracelet—an extravagant and beautiful gift —but under the surface, her smile is worried instead of delighted. Puzzled, I shrug off the notion, determined to enjoy a happy Christmas with my family.

The evening sneaks in to greet us. After we've stuffed our tummies and tidied the kitchen, we enjoy a Christmas story and warm ourselves by the fire. Iris is sent to bed and reminded not to rise until the sun does. Mother's voice reaches us like a soft autumn breeze as she sings Iris to sleep. Father puts another log on the fire and settles in with a cup of tea and a gingersnap.

My eyes become heavy with the warmth of the crackling fire. The scent of pine fills the air, and the weight of a homemade quilt is upon my outstretched legs. Mother tucks the quilt under my chin before she rubs my back and suggests I retire for the evening.

"In a minute," I say. "I'd like to let the warmth soak into my bones a little longer."

Father gets up from his chair with a groan. "Time to hit the hay, Mother?"

Mother takes the cup from his hand. "It's been a full day, for certain." She takes the cup to the washbasin in the kitchen.

"Good night, Violet," Mother calls from the threshold before she walks down the short hallway to her bed.

He kisses my forehead. "Sleep tight, pumpkin."

"Night, Dad." Sleepiness crawls into my voice.

I snuggle deeper into the sofa cushions and pull the quilt along with me. Home feels good, the familiar scents, sights, and sounds. I let the comfort of home permeate me.

Sleep descends upon me, and I dream until a log shifts in the fireplace. A cascade of sparks and crackles erupt into the quiet. I bolt upright. "The letter!" I almost scream before I remember where I am.

I stumble out from under the heavy blanket and brace myself

for balance before I tiptoe to the bedroom that now belongs to Iris. "How could I have forgotten John's letter?" I say under my breath. The door creaks as I enter the room. I poke around in the dark for the bag at the end of my bed. I stub my toe on a raised floorboard and stifle a yelp, tumbling forward onto the mattress. The suitcase sits at the foot of the bed. I search the inside pocket for the letter. Relief washes over me as I retrieve the envelope and retrace my steps to the living room.

Letter in hand, I forgive my forgetfulness, given the merriment of the day. I sit on the edge of my seat cushion and peel open the envelope, careful not to tear the edges. I unfold the letter and a photo drops onto my lap. I hold the picture at eye level, squinting in the near blackness of the room. I tilt the photograph toward the light of the fire, and John's face smiles back at me. He holds a weapon with a long barrel, much like a shotgun, in both hands. There is tall grass behind him, and beyond that is the outline of a round target.

I take my blanket and sit on the floor, wrapped up like a caterpillar in a cocoon, to read by the light of the fire.

SUNDAY, *December 19, 1943*

Dearest Violet,

I was so sorry to hear of your friend's loss. I am sure her sweetheart was a good man and a good soldier. He served his country with bravery. I wish I could be there to hold you tight, to comfort you. My only regret is not being with you all this time. I wish you wouldn't worry, but same as I understand how worry won't change the course of the future, I know that asking you not to worry is only a feeble attempt to make myself feel better. I never meant to cause you this pain. This I pray you do understand.

I hope you received the gift I sent. I don't want to spoil the surprise, in case the package hasn't yet arrived, but I want you to know that the gift reminded me of you. You are the only girl for me, Vi.

I opened your present before the twenty-fifth, but I was eager for news from you. I opened the package this morning after a fitful sleep in which I dreamed of you. I woke early, disgruntled and sleep deprived, then I dressed and left the tent so as not to wake the others. I walked out into the tall grass that lay beyond a hill that overlooks the town, and I sat under a large oak tree and opened your gift. I love the handkerchiefs, with my initials and all. Looks like you spent some time on them. Thank you. They are appreciated. The sweets are a real treat, too. I will have to hide them under my covers so the boys don't get at them. The best surprise though, Vi, the best gift of all was that the box carried your scent. I breathed in so deep I thought you might emerge, like magic. I know the fragrance won't last forever, but to have the sweet smell of your perfume on each handkerchief makes me a truly happy man. I promise to always carry one with me, no matter where I go.

I wanted you to know that I received orders. I am to be shipped out next Tuesday. I don't know where I'll be for Christmas, but in my heart, I will be with you at home. I can't speak much of plans here, so you will have to trust that I will do everything in my power to stay safe. My letters might take a while to reach you, so try not to worry yourself sick. There are no days off in a war, so I'll write when I can. Either way, you are on my mind, in my heart, and on my lips every moment.

Merry Christmas to you and your family. I am healthy and well.

Love, John

I am sick with dread. John isn't where I thought he was. He has already left basic training, and I can't know where he has gone. I clutch my stomach, and the letter crumples against my abdomen.

The room feels too warm. I toss the blanket off, and I stand with an abruptness that surprises my feet. I wobble a little before I march into the kitchen and throw open the back door. I breathe in gulps of air and lean against the doorframe until numbness overtakes me.

I am still in the doorway when Mother comes in, bundled against the cold air that pierces the night. "Violet, what has come over you?"

"Sorry." I shiver.

She closes the door and places her hands on my shoulders. She maneuvers me into the living room and gently pushes me into the chair by the fire.

Mother kneels in front of me and takes my face in her hands. Words tumble out of my mouth as fast as tears fall from my eyes. I tell her about the letter and that I don't know where John is. I divulge how angry I was at him. I tell her about my childish behavior and the unopened letters—with both relief and fear.

Mother's eyes brim with moisture as she rocks me. "This is what I've feared for you, dear. I never wanted you to feel such pain."

We sit cradled in each other's arms. As the tears dry, they leave phantom trails of agony. The night evolves into day. The sun leans its round, luminous body against the horizon, and life begins again.

✳ ✳ ✳

$\mathcal{M}$ ay 4, 1944

THURSDAY AT THE OFFICE, the weather has cooled dramatically, but the promise of a warm weekend has all the Realtors preparing for a busy Saturday of showcasing farms and homes. We have a shortage of signage, so I'm on the phone with the printer, charming my way to a speedy delivery of freshly printed advertising. When he assigned me the task this morning, Jim told me I could charm the pants off anyone. I laughed and admitted that I'd inherited the trait from my father, a man who has worked his charming magic on me from time to time. I hang up the phone, smiling to myself. The signs will be ready tomorrow at two. I make a note on my desk calendar, and when I glance up, I notice a shadow outside.

A bicycle leans against the oversized glass window, causing the glass to rattle in the sill. My breath catches, and a strangled sound emerges from my barely parted lips. I place both palms flat on the desk to steady myself as I stand. The bell above the door jingles. A boy of about seventeen, clothed in the dark uniform of a military messenger, steps toward me with a stiff, unnatural gait.

"I've a telegram for Mrs. Boyd," he says.

I shake my head. "No. Please, no."

"Are you Mrs. Boyd?" He lowers his voice, and his eyes glance downward apologetically. He steps closer and extends the envelope with a nervous smile.

"Violet? What is it, dear?" Mrs. Boyd must have heard the

87

door and my lack of reply. She peeks around the wall that separates her office from the reception area. She steps around to my desk. Mrs. Boyd looks from the messenger to me, and back to the messenger. The color drains from her plump cheeks, leaving an empty paleness that, in seconds, ages her by ten years.

"Ma'am," he says to her, shuffling his feet. "I'm sorry, ma'am, but I have a telegram for Mrs. Boyd."

She purses her lips and frowns. "Thank you, dear. I—I am Mrs. Boyd."

She signs the paper on his clipboard and accepts the letter.

Her gaze lowers to the envelope as the door whispers closed. A dampened jingle from the bell shivers over the room.

A tear slides down her face and meanders along contours of her laugh lines. "I had a bad sense about today." Her shoulders give way to a sob that crumples her body in half. I watch in slow motion as grief fills the space where worry used to live.

Tears spring to my eyes as I round my desk to embrace her now fragile body. She trembles in my arms and lets out a low, guttural howl—a sound that will haunt me forever. This frightens me, what death can do. It can transform a person into an empty shell so they feel nothing and everything at the same time.

I hear Jim's rapid, uneven footsteps on the hard floor before I see him half-running, half-limping toward us. Summoned from his office by the commotion, his face is flushed and full of questions.

The rest of our coworkers begin to gather. They whisper, standing in a semicircle around Mrs. Boyd and me. Little is said as we cling to each other.

"Mrs. Boyd?" Jim touches her shoulder. "What's happened?"

I lift my chin and peer into Jim's troubled face. "She received a telegram." I gasp for a solid breath of air. "From the war office."

Fresh tears fall as Mrs. Boyd convulses in my arms. My body

is no match for the strength with which she mourns. I cannot let go. If I did, I would feel as if I had abandoned her down the darkest pit on earth. So, I hold on, arms burning and back straining. I am all that stands between her, the floor, and her own personal hell.

Jim steps around us and gently extracts the envelope from Mrs. Boyd's grip.

He takes a few staggered steps toward the window. His tall frame casts a shadow over us. The sound of paper tearing echoes through the room.

He sighs, before whispering instructions to a colleague. "Go to the lumberyard and fetch Mr. Boyd. Bring him here at once. Don't tell him any news. Let him know Mrs. Boyd needs him. After that, go find the doc, tell him to bring a sedative to calm her nerves."

The door opens and closes, and Jim directs the others to return to their desks. "Violet, why don't we bring Mrs. Boyd to my office?" He gestures with one arm while the other wraps around Mrs. Boyd's shoulders, guiding her to the quiet office.

Mrs. Boyd sits in the guest chair. I sit beside her and hold tight to her hand while I rub her arm. Jim sets a glass on the desk in front of Mrs. Boyd and pours a bit of dark brown liquid. My nose itches at the smell of bourbon.

"Here. Drink this, Mrs. Boyd." Jim holds out the glass to her. "This will help."

Mrs. Boyd lets go of my hand and cradles the small glass with both palms. The first sip must burn, cutting a path down her throat. Mrs. Boyd shakes her head sharply and then empties the glass, placing it back on the desk with a thud.

We sit in silence as the minutes pass. Mrs. Boyd's distraught eyes stare out the window into the distance. An occasional hiccup escapes her throat as she settles into shock.

My thoughts flow to John. I pray he is all right as I nervously touch the silver heart around my wrist.

Mr. Boyd arrives at the office panicked. Sweat pours down his round, flushed face as he enters Jim's office.

"Jim?" He kneels beside his wife, takes her hands, and searches her face for answers.

"Arthur," Jim says with a sullen voice. "A telegram arrived today. I am sorry to tell you that Paul was killed in action."

I stand to make space for the Boyds to hold each other. Mr. Boyd leans into Mrs. Boyd. They murmur hushed words between sobs.

Jim and I leave the office. The weeping from behind the closed door escalates.

"This breaks my heart," I say. "So pointless. Paul was their only child. How is it fair they should lose him?" Tears sting my eyes. I blink them back as a rush of emotion pools in my belly.

"Life isn't fair, Violet. Life will always have heartache." Jim shakes his head. "What matters is what you do with the heartache. You can wallow or you can move on. Choice is up to you."

Jim's words are true, but the truth is distasteful to me in this moment. I feel the urge to run away, to hide so the war can never touch me or those I hold dear. I want this horrible, frightful war to end, and I want it to end right now.

Exhaustion fills every pore. I find myself seated at my desk, in a blank daze. I remain there all afternoon, unmoving, and stare the nothingness of grief in the eye. The Boyds left over an hour ago. Jim took them out the back door and drove them home. There is little for me to do, and even though I don't want to be here, I already dread being at home, alone with my thoughts.

As four thirty arrives, I decide to make an impromptu visit to the Smith house. I am supposed to meet the girls at the hall for sewing, but I cannot stomach the thought. I don't want to tell them about Paul Boyd. Mrs. Boyd has been the cornerstone of our volunteer duties. She moves about the hall with delightful ease. She flits from one group to another, always ready to lend a hand to help, an ear to listen, or a chuckle to lighten the mood. My heart sinks as I think of the Boyds and am once again ill equipped to assist in any meaningful way.

I am aware that my desire to avoid the girls this afternoon is similar to the way Helen avoided us when she lost Robert. At the time, my only concern was to be a good friend to Helen, to let her know she wasn't alone. But now, I understand that she would have known— no matter how hard I tried to conceal my thoughts —that while I was there to comfort her, I was also thankful that my John was alive and well. Perhaps that pill is a might bit too bitter to swallow. Helen did what she needed to in order to stem the bleeding of her own heart.

This war is a monster. It steals from us in broad daylight, and it snuffs out hope and life. Today, the war has beaten me. I slink toward the Smith house, seeking comfort and a soft place to land, even if only for a little while.

* * *

 une 1, 1944

I sᴛᴏᴘ to collect my mail before climbing the stairs to my apartment. After long days at the office, without Mrs. Boyd's banter to lighten the mood, these two flights of stairs have begun to feel like a long climb up a water tower.

Letters from John are infrequent and short, written on any scrap of paper he can find. My mood has been in a downward spiral since the news of Paul Boyd arrived. I'm aware of the darkness that surrounds me, but I don't know how to address it. Perhaps there is no cure at all. But, I console myself with this awareness all the same. Beth and Lauren visit on a regular basis. They stop by for tea each week after they finish their sewing projects. I haven't been able to force myself to the hall since Paul Boyd's funeral service. My volunteer efforts didn't stop the war, and they didn't bring John home. I soothe my battered ego as I fall for its lies. I'd rather be right than logical, at the moment.

I retrieve the letter from the box and allow myself to feel some relief. He was alive and well enough to write this letter. *But what about today? Is he still alive today?* My shoulders drop as fear takes up residence in my subconscious. These days, dread is in my every thought, my every action. I push the anxiety from my mind and step with heavy legs onto the wooden stairs. The sound reverberates through the hall and through my head.

I toss my purse on the table and sit down. I attempt to settle my nerves with a few slow breaths before I slide my thumb under the flap and unseal the envelope.

WEDNESDAY, May 10, 1944

Dearest Violet,

I hope this letter finds you well. Your letters reach me fine. Though I understand from your correspondence that mine take weeks and sometimes months to reach you.

I was sad to hear of Paul Boyd. A fine young man he was. He made his parents and his country proud. Please offer my condolences to the Boyds. They are kind folk, and I know how fond you are of Mrs. Boyd in particular.

I keep up with a few boys from home, but not as much as I would like. Most days I can hardly find a spare moment to write to you and Mother and Father. We're training pretty hard right now, but I can't say what for. I don't know where we are headed or what we will encounter. Food is mighty good, though, and plenty to go around. They work us all day in the heat, with maneuvers and equipment I've never seen before. They sure push us to our outer limits. But come chow time, we are treated to meals fit for a king. I eat more than my weight in potatoes each night, trying to keep my energy up for the next day. So far, this plan has worked in my favor.

Some boys have already fallen behind in training, and I can't let myself worry about what will happen to them once we're among the enemy.

I've been assigned to a right successful group of men, the First Infantry Division. They have pillaged their way through the war for some time. To tell you the truth, Vi, I suspect we're headed into something big. The air is electric here. Tension fills every vacant space, like the way smoke permeates every crevice of a room when the damper on the fireplace is shut tight. The boys try to downplay the fear, but we all feel the trepidation.

I won't lie to you, Vi. I am scared. I wonder what I will do when I come face to face with the enemy. I know that someone out there wants to kill me, as bad as I am supposed to want to kill them. Truth is, I don't want to kill anyone. I don't want to be the reason someone else's life ends. But, most of all, I'm afraid of becoming someone who no longer knows the difference. Someone numb to the act of war. I don't know who I'd be if that ever happened.

You are always on my mind and in my heart. If I pay close attention, I can remember the softness of your hair and the taste of your sweet red lips. My favorite memory is that day we sat under the big old tree on your daddy's farm. Remember how we listened to the crickets and watched the grass sway with the wind? Sometimes I can feel the sun on my arms and hear your laugh as the prairie dogs peek up from their holes, trying to spy on us as they chattered in their secret code. That memory makes me smile every time, Vi.

I look forward to your next letter. I don't know when I'll be able to write again, but I promise to send another letter as soon as I am able.

In my thoughts and prayers always.

Love,

John

I GLANCE at the calendar and count the days. He wrote this over three weeks ago. I gasp as my chest tries to cave in. He could be anywhere by now. He could be deep in battle with the Germans or the Italians—or the Japanese. My heart drops into my stomach, and out of fear or habit, I pray for his safety.

I wonder if he has written to his parents since. I grab my purse and dash out the door. The Smith home sits at the edge of town, a little over three miles from my apartment. I walk as fast as I can without flailing into a run. The blood pounding in my head spurs my movements. Sweat drips down the sides of my face as I clutch John's letter.

My walk turns to a run as the quaint cottage style house comes into view. Mother Smith is in the front garden, digging with a hand shovel. "Violet, dear. What brings you by?"

"A letter. A letter from John arrived." My words are halted by my breathlessness.

Mother Smith wipes her dirt stained hands on her apron as she steps out of the shade to greet me. "A letter? Violet dear, did you run all this way?"

I shake my head and the motion makes me feel nauseated. I stumble, one hand clutching my stomach while the other reaches for my sweat covered forehead.

Mother Smith's expression changes from pleasant to worried, right before I feel myself leaning. I grapple for the porch railing, and everything goes black.

"*S*he'll be fine. Really, Liz. The doctor has already come and gone. Fainted is all." Mother Smith's voice drifts through the house. My eyes, narrow slits, take in the furniture of the Smiths' living room. "Of course you are welcome to come, but we'll keep her here overnight, just to make sure. No trouble at all. Okay, I will talk to you in the morning. Bye."

My hand moves to my forehead, where I find a cool, wet cloth. "You're awake." Mother Smith peers down at me. "How are you feeling?"

"Tired, I guess. Did I really faint?"

"Yes, dear. Not to worry at all. Doc says you'll be good as new in no time." Mother Smith kneels beside the sofa and places a cool palm to my cheek.

I notice her other hand is wrapped in gauze. "What happened to your hand?"

"Scraped against the railing when I reached out to catch you. A little scrape is all. I'll be dandy." She smiles.

"You caught me? Thank you," I stammer. The thought of Mother Smith catching me sends a shiver of embarrassment through my body.

"I wasn't going to watch you fall."

"Was that Mother on the phone?" I ask.

"Yes, I called her as soon as the doctor left. Everything is already sorted. You'll stay the night with us, and Father will return you to town once you're up and around."

I offer a feeble, "Thank you."

"Grief can trap you in the underbelly of mankind, you know. No person should spend too much time there. The soul cannot withstand a life lived in grief." Mother Smith putters about the living room, finally settling herself on a stool near the sofa.

Tears prickle in the corners of my eyes. My voice is solemn and vacant. "I don't know what to do with all this sadness."

"Sadness has a time and a place. It serves a purpose, allows us to get by and it can make us stronger. But you, dear Violet. You need to move past the sadness and reclaim your life."

"How do I do that?" I roll onto my side to face John's mother.

"You decide to move forward is all." A kind, knowing smile spreads across her face. "And you eat. Look at you, skin and bones. No wonder you fainted. This we can fix." She pats my arm and heads toward the kitchen.

As Mother Smith moves about the kitchen, I think, *What do I do, if John doesn't come back?* The question looms like a dark cloud until exhaustion finds me again.

I fall in and out of sleep as the Smith family meanders about the house. Mother Smith feeds me chicken soup and fresh bread with butter. Edward, curious at three years old, sneaks into the living room to visit me, often enough to be admonished by his mother.

The sky grows dark, and the house's chatter begins to subside. Edward's bedtime is announced, but before he is captured and escorted to bed, he makes his way to my side and places a soft, wet, gentle kiss atop my forehead. "Good night, Vi."

I smile, a tear rolling down my cheek. John is the only person in this world who calls me Vi. All I can figure is Edward learned from the best.

✳✳✳

 une 5, 1944

THE SUN SHINES in the clear sky. The light wind moves at the pleasant speed of a caterpillar, barely a whisper. I don't know whether the summer temperature has caused my delighted mood or if I am finally coming back to myself.

Today marked my return to the Production Corps. Lauren and Beth were thrilled to see me and caused such a ruckus that Mrs. Beattie stepped in to quieten the reunion, though she did so with a slight smile upon her lips.

After sewing, we celebrate at the Fountain with milkshakes, French fries, and apple pie.

Music plays in the background as Lauren dips her French fry into mustard, her signature move.

"I think we should make a plan," Beth says, scrunching her nose at Lauren's mustard antics.

"What kind of a plan?" I sip my thick strawberry shake.

"One that keeps us on the right side of this unrest." Beth shrugs.

"Keep each other healthy, happy, and together?" Lauren asks.
"Yeah. Like that." Beth says.
By the end of the evening, we have planned activities to keep our spirits up. We've promised to share our sweethearts' letters and to be honest with one another, even when we can't be honest with ourselves. But we've also agreed that, depending on the

situation, we may have to tell half truths to keep one another afloat. Our plan morphs into a life raft, and as we say goodbye, we forge a stronger bond, one that can withstand chaos, war, and even, if need be, death.

FRIDAY, May 26, 1944

Dearest Violet,

I hope this letter finds you well. This may be my last chance to write for some time. Activity is heating up, and though nothing specific has been said, I can feel the pressure building, like when the air changes before we see the storm coming across the prairie sky. We are in a holding pattern, but I suspect the day will arrive soon.

I am in love with the coast of England and hope to bring you here one day. The ruggedness has lit a fire deep within me, and I want nothing more than to share the experience with you. I know you would appreciate the region as much as I do, Vi.

We are now surrounded by hordes of British and American ships. The villagers must feel like they have already been invaded, rather than protected. Men in uniforms dominate the region. I am keeping well, and my strength is good. My shoulders have almost doubled in size since I left Cedar Springs.

Thank you for the photo. You look beautiful as ever. I was in need of a replacement, as the previous photo has taken a beating. I pull it out of my pocket several times a day.

We are mighty and we are strong. I believe we can win this war, after all.

You are in my thoughts and prayers always.

Love,

John

* * *

 une 6, 1944

THE RADIO PLAYS SOFTLY in the living room. I share the news from John, and the Smiths allow me to read the letter he sent them. We talk about the length of time between his letters and the secrecy about his special training. We theorize about what type of mission he might be involved in and invent stories of Allied troops swooping into Berlin. The stories are bittersweet, and we can taste the difference. Though we all are desperate to win the war, the necessary means sticks in our throats.

We reminisce late into the evening, telling stories from childhood up to John's last day in Cedar Springs. Mother Smith remembers him as a quiet, soulful boy, who preferred a tranquil spot among the trees to the activity of the town center. She talks about his sweet nature as a young child, telling tales of generosity and kindness.

Father Smith tells about John's fishing excursions. "He is a fabulous fisherman," he says proudly. "He is patient as the day is long. He caught fish on almost every outing he went on." Father Smith pauses as he pats his wife's knee. "He never brought a single fish home, though, not until I asked him."

"What? What do you mean?" I ask.

"He threw them all back, told me he couldn't stand to end the life of a fish. After I told him that eating the fish was as much a part of the experience as casting the rod, he brought home a fish every three or four times he went out." Father Smith chuckles. "I think he started bringing them back just to please me. He is a good boy, without a doubt."

"He threw them all back?" I never knew that about John. *What did he think war was going to be like?*

I settle myself on the sofa with a blanket and pillow and spend the rest of the night awake, pondering the delightful and amusing mysteries of John Smith.

***

*J*une 7, 1944

"CBS WORLD NEWS REPORTING. We interrupt this program to bring you the latest on the Allied effort. Berlin radio is reporting that an Allied infiltration, which they are calling 'the Invasion,' has hit German troops in the northern region of France's coastline. Although several German radio stations are reporting on this attack by Allied forces, there are still no reports from the Allied Force Headquarters in London. We remind you that Germany is indeed capable of this kind of psychological warfare, and until confirmation arrives from Allied Headquarters, all reports must be viewed as unconfirmed."

The news arrived in the wee hours of the morning, after I had succumbed to a fitful sleep. I become aware of the commotion when I arrive at the office. Jim and the others gather around the radio and tilt their ears toward the static.

First, the news trickles in from German radio sources. Once confirmed in a live broadcast by General Eisenhower, Supreme Commander of the Allied Forces, the news of the attack floods the radio airwaves. Excitement builds in the office, and everyone cheers as the announcement is translated into different languages for all of Europe. Giddiness fills the air as we hug, laugh, and cry at the news. The Allied Forces are on their way to victory.

Little business takes place as we all hover over the radio. Beyond the large picture window, the town streets are alive with uncertain but hopeful faces.

I step outside the back door. I need to say a prayer for John. Right now, my prayers are the only way I can help him. I know he is in that force. He is fighting through France, and I can't help but think we may win the war, but I may lose John.

I wipe a rogue tear from my eye, jut my chin forward, and hold my arms tight at my sides, hands curled into fists. I must stay strong and believe he will be safe. I will hold that as my new truth. I will not let fear delude me. I will not let this war beat me down any longer. I am strong. I am capable. I am the one John clings to and I to him.

I open the door and step inside the hallway.

"There you are," Jim says. "Mr. Smith is here to see you. He ran all the way from the bakery."

I find Mr. Smith immersed in excited conversation with another Realtor.

"Violet," he says, out of breath but exuberant. "Can you believe the news? This is what John wrote about. A real attack. One that'll show those Germans what we are made of."

I smile at him, sweet as ever, enthusiastic face dusted with flour. "Sure is incredible news. That is for certain."

"I'm running home now, got to tell the missus. She doesn't put the radio on till the evening, you know. She'd be sour as a crab apple if I didn't tell her what our John was up to. We are gonna win this war, Violet. John will come home. You'll see."

"Yes. Yes, he will." I am surprised that I, too, am willing to embrace this notion. Fresh tears, but happy ones, spring to my eyes as Mr. Smith wraps me in a quick hug before he grasps the door handle and runs down the street to spread the news.

***

*J*anuary, 1945

THE HOLIDAYS COME AND GO. I sent a package to John, filled with sweet treats, homemade jam from Mother, and a fresh batch of handkerchiefs sprayed with my favorite perfume. I hope my gift reached him, though I have not received any correspondence since before Christmas. He apologized for being unable to send a gift.

The few letters I have received over the last several months are polite and kind, but I sense a shift in him, one I can only blame on the war. I know this time away has cost him a piece of himself. He doesn't tell me of the horrors he has seen, and for now, I respect his decision. There will be time enough to heal when he comes home. "When he comes home," I murmur.

I leave the apartment and stop at the mailbox on my way to the office. I place another letter into the slot for pickup and slide on my mittens before I step outside into the frigid air.

MONDAY, January 29, 1945

Dear John,

I hope this letter finds you healthy, safe, warm, and fed. I haven't received a letter from you in some time, but I do hope you are receiving mine. I will continue to write every few days in the hopes that a few will reach you.

Your mother and father are both fine, as are your siblings.

I'm sure you'll be surprised by how much little Edward has grown. I suppose I should stop calling him "little" now that he's at my waist. He still prefers to sit on my knee, though, when we listen to radio programs or when I read to him. He remains the cuddly one of the bunch.

Work at the office continues as usual. We spend most days with the radio on now. The news bulletins keep us up to date with how the Allied troops are managing. I'm not sure if you hear news of what happens elsewhere in the war. Allied troops are moving forward and victory is within reach. I think of all the people displaced from their homes, of them and their children hiding in the woods, and I thank God you are putting those atrocities right. You're giving them back their homes, their lives, and their country. You are a brave and fearless man, John Smith, and I couldn't be prouder of you.

I almost forgot to tell you that Jim, from the office, is engaged to be married. Can you believe that? The old bachelor is exchanging his one room apartment for a home with his love.

He and Frances plan to wed in late spring, after the ground has thawed. He purchased a small home a few blocks from the office. They plan to host the reception there, as the garden will be in full bloom. This wedding is one of the rare happy events that I look forward to. Jim is beside himself with glee, and Frances is such a lovely girl. I'd be honored if you would attend as my date. Given that spring is still a ways off, I am hopeful you will be home to join me.

I'd better warm some soup before I turn in. Please be safe and know that you are loved.

All my love,
Violet

I MEET Lauren and Beth for tea at the Fountain after work. We see each other almost every day now, and I have grown to love these two women like sisters. We sip our tea and nibble on a plate of onion rings. We tell each other about work and family and share details of our sweethearts' letters. We giggle like schoolgirls, our voices climbing above the diner's music. These are the moments we strive to create. We need to find a bit of normal and to keep our spirits up so we can stay strong for those overseas.

I am in the middle of a story about Edward's shenanigans when Helen enters the diner. I pause mid sentence as my eyes meet hers. My mouth falls open, and I gape at her frail body, her dress hanging limply from her frame.

"Helen." I search my brain for an appropriate comment, unable to take my eyes off her sunken cheeks. "Good to see you."

Helen walks to our table. She doesn't light up with a smile, but she doesn't frown at us either, which I take as a good sign.

"Helen," both Lauren and Beth squeal in unison.

Helen looks out of place as she twists the handle of her purse between both hands. "Hello. Nice to see you."

"Please sit." I slide over to make room, though unnecessary for her skeletal frame.

"No," she says. A sharp tone cuts through her willowy voice. "Thanks." Her eyes drop to her shoes, and I sense that she would rather be anywhere but here.

"Helen, please. Join us," Lauren says. "We haven't seen you in ages, and we want you to know we are here for you."

Helen nods with a brisk tilt of her head toward the door. "I'm only here because Mother made me come."

"You aren't up to a visit yet?" I ask, in a soft soothing tone, like she were a frightened animal.

"To be honest," she says, a stricken expression creeping over her hollow face, "I'm not up for much these days."

She offers a weak smile before she pivots on her heel, brushes past her mother and escapes out the door.

We sit and stare at our fingernails for what feels like an eternity before Beth clears her throat. "Robert passed a year ago. I don't think she is herself yet."

"I'm worried for her," Lauren says.

"I've known Helen since high school," I say. "She could be a little solemn, but I've never seen her so unhinged." I choke up as a familiar thought enters my mind. "Promise me you won't let me get that way if John doesn't come home."

"Never." Beth searches my eyes.

"Of course not," Lauren says. "We wouldn't let that happen."

I nod and cling to their words of encouragement. Our pact is to keep each other strong, no matter what. Even when that means lying to keep us sane.

* * *

 ebruary 1945

A WEEK and a half after our encounter with Helen, Mrs. Beattie enters the sewing room. She closes the door behind her and apologizes for the interruption. "Helen was found early this morning," she says. "She drowned in the semi frozen lake on the Parker property. Her and Robert's favorite picnic spot." Her lip quivers. "It is undetermined whether her death was accidental. All I know is she was found cloaked in Robert's favorite sweater, one his mother knit for him."

Mrs. Beattie's tough outer shell cracks as she hugs each of us. A sob escapes from her lips, and she retreats to the common room, leaving us to deal with yet another blow from this wretched war.

The news of Helen hits each of us differently, and yet the blow strikes our core. Lauren, nervous by nature, turns her attention to the sewing machine, out of desire to keep her hands moving, I suspect. Beth, a devout Catholic, finds a corner of the room and prays for Helen's soul. The drumming of the sewing machine mixed with Beth's murmuring electrify the uneasiness within me. The horrid thoughts questioning my inner strength surface like lily pads in an overcrowded pond.

We all need to collect ourselves, so we retire early from sewing and promise to meet again the next evening.

Tea at the diner is replaced by sewing at the hall. We meet every night. We have little to say, but we are determined to be present for each other and for Helen. Our love for one another remains, though our paths through this unchartered water take us deep into our own thoughts. We attempt to make sense of our own grief, while also trying to dissect Helen's. Most often, I am either questioning my sanity or deep in prayer, not only for John's safe return, but also for Helen's soul.

The funeral is set for a week after her death. The three of us gather at the graveside, keenly aware that the pit of despair now lies a bit closer to each of us. Grief exhausts us, and after Helen's funeral, we collapse on my sofa. We lean against one another in comfortable silence and remain there while the afternoon passes. None of us want to be alone on this day, yet we aren't quite ready for real life to begin.

These past two weeks have felt like months. They drag by while I put on a brave face, as I imagine Mother would do. Helen never did that. She never pretended to be okay. Maybe the pretending is what eventually makes life manageable. Or maybe I am delusional and am in as much trouble as Helen was. I hope to never know which is true.

* * *

 ebruary 23, 1945

FRIDAY SWEEPS in to greet me before I can grab hold of the week. Jim kindly allowed me a few days to gather myself, but I'm returning to work today. I've wandered about my apartment in a fog since the funeral, so this morning I am panicked as I pack my overnight bag for a weekend with the Smith family. I run out the door, bag in hand, determined to leave the grief behind and arrive at work on time.

The radio plays news in the background as I file papers and answer phone calls. The radio has become such a constant companion to our workday that I often tune out the noise. My ears only come alive when a song I am fond of airs.

The day is chilly. I make several cups of tea, and before I am aware, the winter sun has set. As I prepare the office to close for the weekend, I hum along to Bing Crosby's "Don't Fence Me In." My imagination conjures the image of John and me together on a front porch, surrounded by children and farmland.

I continue to hum the song as I walk to the Smith house, moving with purpose to stave off the winter frost. In times like these, I allow myself to dream. My dreams help me cling to the notion that John will return safe and sound. At the moment, the dream is all I have. There has been no correspondence from John since before the holidays, but instead of worrying over the silence, I heed his advice from a previous letter. "Don't go worrying yourself sick," he wrote. "Worrying won't change the future, but praying sure might." A smile lingers on my lips as I think of the nononsense way he conveys facts he feels to be common sense. He never skirted around a point, so I take his words to heart, along with everything else he ever told me.

Friday evening at the Smith house begins with tea in the living room as Mother Smith and I catch up on news from town. These days, the dialogue is often fraught with sadness as we learn of another neighbor lost to the war effort. Though we never utter the words, I'm certain we both thank God that John is not the topic of conversation. We talk about the tragedy of Helen's death and how the funeral was even sadder, with only Helen's mother, Robert's parents, Lauren, Beth, and myself in attendance.

My mood lightens as I play with Edward before dinner. His preference is often a book or the Chutes and Ladders game he got from Santa. I am invigorated by Edward's four-year-old enthusiasm for life. He lives from moment to moment with little thought of the past or future. Childlike banter is a blessing, one I cherish in these heavy days.

Watching him play, I am reminded of Iris's joyful self expression. Though at fifteen going on sixteen, I think the time has long since passed for her to step into the role of a young lady, a role she resists with enthusiasm. Mother's persuasions, like mine, have had little impact on her. Our last discussion on the topic resulted in a heated debate, which left a wedge between us. Sometimes I wish I could adopt her carefree nature, even for a little while. I'd like to feel her ease about the world around her.

I head into the kitchen to work alongside Mother Smith and John's sisters as we prepare dinner. I often share my leftover rations with the family. I can stretch a pound of butter with ease, but for a large family with children still on the grow, rations are trickier to manage.

After dinner, we shoo John's parents to the living room to enjoy their evening tea, and his sisters and I clean up the dishes. I am happy to help with the chores, as their including me in their family has been a welcomed experience. This time, too, is precious. The three of us discuss the latest movie pictures, radio broadcasted soap operas, and of course, the local boys they happen to be fawning over at the time. They are still young enough to be wrapped up in their own teenage worlds, but aware enough to know the real world is a bundle of change. They treat me like an older sister, and I dole out advice, only when asked, never overstepping my role in their lives.

With the kitchen tidy, we join the rest of the family in the living room. Father Smith switches on the radio, and our favorite evening broadcast begins. Edward snuggles beside me on the sofa, and the minutes fly by as we listen to the antics of Fibber McGee and Molly.

Tonight's episode has Fibber McGee determined to tune the family piano. His efforts have little success, however his attempts elicit laughter and applause. When the musical interlude begins, Edward jumps down from the sofa and thuds against the floor on two flat feet. He pulls his mother's hands to hoist her out of her chair, and they dance around the room while the rest of us watch and clap to the music.

With the Smith children all tucked in, Father Smith turns the radio on once more. The three of us sit huddled closer to the fire and listen for updates from the war office.

"World News Today. This is CBS News reporting. Earlier this evening, around eight o'clock Eastern War Time, we received a bulletin reading, and I quote, 'The war authority is confirming that the U.S. First Infantry Division has successfully attacked and fractured the Siegfried Line and have fought across the Rur River.' The Rur River flows through Belgium, Germany, and the Netherlands, however ninety percent of the river is situated within German borders. This is another giant step forward in the Allied effort to gain control of German occupied regions."

"First Infantry Division?" I say. "That—that could be John."

"Did they say any casualties?" Mother Smith kneels in front of the radio. If she could, I imagine she would crawl inside the radio to get a little closer to her son. I know how she feels. The butterflies in my heart flap their wings in rapid succession.

"Hush, Mother." Father Smith raises the radio volume.

We listen for another hour, before Father Smith shuts off the broadcast. "No more news tonight, I'm afraid." He guides John's mother, exhausted from worry, toward bed.

$$* \, * \, *$$

$\mathcal{M}$ arch 2, 1945

ANOTHER WEEK PASSES, though the hours feel longer than they used to. Every day this week, I have tucked my lunch under my arm and braced myself against the frigid winter air. I walk the four blocks to the bakery to meet Father Smith as his workday ends. He has visited the war office every day this week, seeking news of John. Little information has been available, and I balance the dreadful task of deciding where frustration ends and outright terror begins. Yesterday, the war office directed him to speak with the Red Cross. Perhaps they would have the time and resources to determine John's status.

Though I will see the Smiths this evening, I don't have the patience to wait another four hours for news of John. My prayers battle each other as I walk, chin stuffed into the warmth of my collar. I crave information, any kind of update. But I know that not all news is welcome.

Father Smith sees me approach the building through the bakery window and greets me at the door. He pulls me in from the cold and shuts the door behind me. The smell of fresh baked bread embraces me. He places a fresh slice of bread into my mitten covered hand, and my tummy rumbles in response.

Hunger wins out over politeness. My teeth sink into the soft bread. I tear at the browned crust, still warm from the oven. "What did the Red Cross say?" I ask with my mouth full.

"They did some preliminary research before I arrived. The war office had notified them I would be on my way." He reaches for another slice of bread from the counter. "All they can say for certain is that John is missing." The news hangs in the air before he hands me the other slice of bread.

"Missing? What does that mean?"

"I suppose they don't know. Day to day operations are chaotic over there." He shrugs. "Troops are moving about. The situation is changing at an even faster rate now than before they crossed the Rur. They promised to keep a lookout for him, but they said no news should be considered good news, at least for now."

My heart sinks and my legs tremble. I brace myself against the window's ledge. I hadn't considered *missing* as an answer to my questions. I shake my head to my illusions, acutely aware of how much is beyond my control.

I feel Father Smith's concerned eyes on me as he surveys the damage this news has done.

I thank him for his time, the bread, and the information and gather myself enough to abate his worry. My hunger evaporates and I leave the bakery still holding the second slice of bread.

The walk back to the office, though just as bitter, is slow as I try to make sense of this new knowledge.

M arch 9, 1945

I STUFF down the panic that rises within me at the slightest thought of John. We have been able to discern little from the radio broadcasts, though I am aware that the reports won't say, "John Smith, safe and forging ahead." We take solace in the knowledge that the Allied troops move forward in what we are told is successful progress. I have a difficult time reconciling the notion of *progress* and *war* in one sentence. Neither word is suited for the other, in my opinion.

When I arrive at work Friday morning, Jim is leaning on my desk, newspaper in hand.

"Did you see this?" He holds the paper above his head.

"See what?" I hang my bright green spring jacket on the hook.

Jim reads aloud from the paper. "'Allied army across Rhine.'

They've done it, Violet. They've captured a bridge and are moving deep into German territory. We're almost there. I can feel victory in my bones." His grin is wide and contagious.

I reach for the paper and read the first few paragraphs before I return the pages to him. "Good news, I suppose." I'm uncertain whether I should try to convince Jim or myself. Without contact from John, the days are challenging to navigate.

Jim's face adjusts in response to my lack of excitement. "No news?"

"No news," I say. "War office won't confirm or deny. Red Cross still doesn't know much, but they're looking into his whereabouts for the Smiths. Mr. Smith has been down at their office every lunch hour for almost two weeks." I shrug and try to shake off my worry. "No news is good news. At least that is what they tell me."

"You all right? I mean, you holding up and all?" Concern edges into the lines around Jim's eyes.

"I'm well as I should be. Word is they lost many in the Ardennes Forest, but I imagine quite an effort is required to sort out who is alive and all that." My voice trembles. I shuffle papers around my desk until Jim gets the idea that I am all out of small talk. Or any other kind of talk for that matter.

I go through each day in a daze. I whisper to myself the mantra I have held dear since receiving John's last letter before Christmas. "John is healthy and well." I repeat my affirmation with a little more intensity. "John is healthy and well." I take a deep breath and calm myself as uncertainties try to sneak past my sturdy guard, and I repeat once more, "John is healthy and well."

The calamities of war have put me on a path from one horrific experience to another. Each time, I am certain that I have now found the most difficult aspect of life amidst war—until another new circumstance presents itself, far worse than anything I have ever known. This pattern repeats as I survive this life consumed by war. Right now, the waiting for life to begin again is what I deem the hardest of all hardships. And so I wait.

*M*ay 7, 1945

THE NEWS FILTERS in over the radio airways. "Germany has surrendered unconditionally." Though we're still waiting for confirmation from the White House or the Allied Headquarters in London, celebrations begin all over town. This must be the most excitement filled Monday I have ever experienced. Strangers run up to me on the street and hug me as we share in the liberation. The streets are crowded, and radios have been moved closer to windows and doorways so the news echoes throughout the alleyways and over the rooftops. Joy and relief flood the streets, reaching everyone within earshot.

Lauren, standing in front of her family's hardware store, sees me from across the street. She waves and dashes through the crowd to meet me. She hugs me with such force that I feel as though I might be crushed. "Isn't this grand news?"

"Incredible," I say, though I'm aware my voice conveys other emotion. "What do you expect will happen now?"

"I don't know. I can't even imagine past this moment. After all we've been through, Violet, we have to let this soak in so no matter what happens, we'll remember that hope existed on this day."

"Hope exists." I squeeze her hands in mine.

We hug again and promise to meet at the diner on Wednesday.

Jim is dancing around the office with Frances. The radio in

the doorway booms at full volume. Each time the announcer speaks, the window rattles against the sill.

"Violet!" Jim grabs my hand and pulls me into their dance. "We've beaten the Germans. I told you I could feel victory. We've won." He spins us around until we tumble against the office furniture, dizzy with relief.

We laugh as we collect ourselves. I smooth my hair into place and head toward my desk.

"No. Not today," Jim says with an authoritative tone. His words tumble out faster than I can register them. "The office is closed. In fact, we will close for the week. Go. See your family. Celebrate with John's. Go to a movie. Heck, I don't care what you do. Promise me you won't come in to work this week. Don't you worry about your pay. You'll still earn your weekly salary. I insist that we all take this time to live a little. This might not be a complete victory, but we're halfway there. That has to be worthy of celebration. Can you do that? For me?"

"Why yes, Jim." I wrap him into a hug fit for an older brother. "I can do that for all of us. Thank you."

I step outside the office and pause to consider where I should go first.

"Violet."

I hear my name but cannot place the caller within the noisy mass of people scattered about the street.

I scan the crowd until I see him. Father is dodging people, making his way toward me. "Violet, I was on my way to collect you. We're all to meet at the church. Come on now."

Unable to hold a conversation with all the commotion, I hug him tight before we venture into the throng of overjoyed town folk.

There is only standing room by the time Father and I arrive. Mother and Iris are seated alongside the Smith family. I wave and catch Iris's eye.

"Today is a day of celebration." Reverend Campbell's

booming voice captures everyone's attention. "Though a celebration of such magnitude does not come without loss, and for those who left this earth far too soon, we pray for their souls."

A stifled cry squeaks out from a pew to my left and I see Mrs. Boyd, supported by Mr. Boyd. My heart lurches. Nothing, not even an end to war, can repair the damage left in its wake.

My thoughts go to John, and I plead with God to tell me he is safe. Then, I decide better of it and instead call on the bravery I have lacked and pray for whatever outcome God wants me to know. Whatever the news, I will adapt. I will heal. I will learn to walk without fear. I will learn to live again.

"I call on you, as a congregation, to continue your prayers for those yet to return. The war in Europe may be over, but our boys are not yet home safe in our arms." Reverend Campbell is moved to song. "Amazing grace, how sweet the sound that saved a wretch like me."

The congregation sways and sings, and I can't help but notice that the sun outside shines a little brighter through the arched windows of the church. A glimmer of hope is sparked within my chest, and my butterflies take flight.

***

*M*ay 31, 1945

SATURDAY, *May 12, 1945*

Dearest Violet,

I hope this letter finds you well. I imagine you have heard the fortunate news that the war, at least in Europe, is over. These past five months have been a grind. There was little time or tools to write, and for that I apologize. We had made such good headway that our orders were to stay the course. We just had to keep on. We had those Germans on the run, Vi, and it was a good thing we didn't stop, or we might not be celebrating this victory.

Know that you were never far from my thoughts, and for that I will be forever in your debt. You pulled me through this filthy, stench infested, miserable war. I'm not sure what will happen next, but for the most part, the fighting has stopped. Some say we'll be sent to England. Others say we are to seek medical attention elsewhere. Not to worry, love, I'm not injured. A military precaution is all. A little R and R would be most welcomed by all of us.

I don't have much time, as I need to get this letter out with the military mail. I want you to know I am healthy and well, and as always, you are in my heart and on my mind. Please give my love to Mother and Father. I promise to write them as soon as I can.

Love, John

. . .

THIS IS the news I have been desperate for. I sit at the bottom of the stairs. My knees shake as I breathe in gulps of air. Relief runs through my blood, and my body shivers. He's alive. He is really alive. I laugh and call out for anybody who is near, "John is alive!"

I slam the mailbox shut and run into the street. I don't stop running until I've reached the Smith house. Mother Smith must have seen me from the window, because she is already on the front steps. "Violet dear, what is it?" Her voice is stretched thin with worry, and I am glad to give her good news.

"He's alive!" I laugh with hysteria. "John's alive."

Her eyes squeeze shut. She holds tight to my shoulders as I tell her all I know.

"Thank the Lord," she says. "He's alive!"

She hollers out again, louder this time, and I see Father Smith running toward us at full speed.

"Mother?" He gasps for air as he reaches her side.

"He's alive. John's alive."

They collapse into each other's arms, laughing and crying. I step back and allow them some space. Happiness fills my every pore as the family I have come to love as my own begins to come alive again right before my eyes.

$$* * *$$

*S*aturday, March 2, 1946

TODAY HAS BEEN LONG OVERDUE. I stand in front of my bedroom mirror and smooth out the pleats in my skirt. The sleet outside my window, though messy and unpleasant, can't touch the joy vibrating inside me.

I paint my lips with my favorite color of red, certain to leave a mark on a worthy cheek. I smile at my reflection and run the brush through my wavy hair once more.

A knock at my door hurries me into action. I mist the air above me with perfume and let the scent cascade over me.

I grab my jacket and purse off the bed and bound to the door.

"Hello, darling. All set?" Father guides my arms into my jacket sleeves.

"I've never been more ready in my life."

"Shall we go see a man about a horse?" He extends his elbow for me to take.

We arrive at the train station—Father, Mother, Iris, and myself. The station is crowded with other anxious townsfolk. The crowd hums with electric conversation as everyone waits for their loved ones to arrive.

I scan the crowd for the Smith family. Ten months ago, I thought John would be home, safe in my arms within a month or two. Though the Germans surrendered to the Allied forces in early May and to the Russians a few days after that, the Japanese decided to fight on, dragging out the messy and arduous war for several more months at the cost of many more lives. When mid-August arrived, the Japanese agreed to an unconditional surrender, and on September 2, 1945, the agreement was formalized and World War II was officially over.

John's letters became more frequent as he left Germany and returned to England for rest, recuperation, and other service details. I breathed much easier with letters arriving every other day. Once he finished his service in England, John informed me that he would travel to the east coast of America on a ship that was to carry German prisoners of war. How odd that must be, I thought, to sit alongside the men who he, only a few months before, had been at war against.

Today, though, is the most wonderful day of all. His letter arrived seven days ago confirming that he would be on the train scheduled to pull into this station at one o'clock. This will be the first time he has set foot on South Dakota soil in almost three years. I am so full of excitement, I feel as if I might burst. I fan myself with both hands. Despite the cold temperature, my cheeks are flamed red with anticipation.

I turn in a circle, searching for the Smiths. "Where could they be?" I mutter. Father tugs on my sleeve, and I follow his gaze to the double doors at the front of the building as Mother Smith, holding Edward's hand, strides toward us. She's almost dragging poor Edward behind her. Father Smith and John's sisters follow behind in quick succession. The breath I've had a hold on whooshes past my lips in relief.

"So sorry we are late." Mother Smith hugs me and then my mother, then embraces Iris in a sideways squeeze. "You'd think all our boys are due home on this particular train, given how busy the streets are."

The floorboards vibrate. Nothing too noticeable, a slight tremor is all. I hesitate, wondering if all I feel is my own nervous energy. Through the little window in the airless station, I see the faint wisps of smoke.

"The train is here!" I shout, which catches the attention of everyone around me.

The short walk through the building to the platform is a maze. I excuse myself and snake around people gathered about the station. The sour weather doesn't deter me from stepping onto the uncovered wooden planks and angling myself to stare into the face of the oncoming train. I forget that I've spent hours on my hair and let the crisp breeze blow my waves around. The dampness seeps through my shoes and bites at the ends of my toes. Nothing will convince me to take my eyes off this train.

I want only to see his face smile at me, for his eyes to meet my own and know we are all safe. I've prepared myself for this moment. I know his family is first in line to welcome him home, so I will be polite and stand to the side to wait my turn to be greeted. I feel both of our families settle in behind me. They chatter as I watch in anticipation for the first glimpse of him.

The train slows to a stop with the squeal of metal on metal before belching out a final plume of smoke.

I survey the tiny windows, but the light's reflection won't allow me to see past the grimy glass. The platform is crowded as people jockey for space. They nudge one another, eager to unite with their loved ones. Passengers disembark, and the crowd erupts with hollers and cheers as men clad in military uniforms step off the train and are embraced by their families.

John stands in the open doorway and waits for the line of passengers to move forward. He looks up for a brief moment, squinting into the brightness. His eyes meet mine and a lopsided smile spreads across his lips. In that split second, I feel John's love surround me.

Before I have the chance to collect myself, to step back and let his mother greet her son, he's wrapped me up. His strong arms swallow me, and he lifts me off my feet and spins me around. He places my feet back on the ground and squeezes me tight once more before he kisses me on the cheek. As he releases me from his embrace, his lips brush mine, so briefly I question whether there was a kiss at all, before thinking of the appropriateness of such a kiss in front of our families.

I feel the heat in my cheeks dissipating as John locks his mother in a long and teary hug. John's sisters join in the hug like a huddle in a football game, while Father Smith hooks his arm around John's shoulders. Edward, still small enough to weave through the crowded legs of his family, captures John's attention by tugging on his pant leg. Everyone steps back as John picks up his younger brother and cradles him like a toddler, despite his growth over the past three years.

Tears of joy trickle down my face as I watch this happy reunion. John shakes my father's hand, kisses my mother on the cheek, and nudges Iris like he would a kid sister.

Without hesitation, he rotates to face me. He has a peculiar look that I can't quite place. With a swift motion, he pulls a box from his pocket and kneels before me on the rain sodden platform planks. "Violet Sanderson." He looks into my eyes. "Will you do me the honor of becoming Mrs. Smith?" He opens the box, revealing a silver band with a single diamond at its center.

My hand flies to my open mouth. "Yes," I say, almost at a whisper. I nod up and down. "Yes."

John slides the diamond onto my left hand. I am still staring at the ring as he cups my face in his hands and tilts my chin. He kisses me with an intensity that is both new and long overdue.

✳ ✳ ✳

*S*aturday, June 8, 1946

THOUGH THE DAY began with a light drizzle, the afternoon skies are blue and cloudless. Iris is fussing with my veil in the bedroom we used to share, while Mother and Father fret about the house.

"I am really happy for you, Violet." Iris places her hands on my shoulders and gives me a squeeze.

"You're always happy," I say, adding a more appropriate, "Thank you."

In the mirror, I see Iris tilt her head, a quizzical expression unfolding over her face. "Did it ever occur to you that I am happy because I choose to be? I won't allow others to cloud my enjoyment of life." Iris steps in front of me and meets my eyes. "You taught me that."

I can't help but laugh. "How did I teach you that?"

"When you were sick with scarlet fever." She pauses as her head tilts to one side. "And every day since then, I suppose. Don't you remember how strong you were? How determined you were to not only survive but to thrive? I've admired you so for your strength,

Violet. You and Mother taught me to be strong enough to go after what I wanted. I wanted to be happy, so I am."

Happy tears dampen my eyes, and I pull Iris into a hug.

Iris speaks softly. "Even you get to choose how you experience life, Violet. Maybe now is the time to choose happiness, too."

128

Iris's words reach deep within me, and I realize Iris has been growing up right before me, all this time.

✳ ✳ ✳

*A*pril 1949

CALLA BABBLES AWAY at the edge of the garden. Two years and one month old, she is a happy child, content to play with her doll on the blanket I've stretched out for her. Bending has become all but impossible for me with my growing baby belly, so I kneel to pull rogue weeds from our little plot of dirt.

The warm spring air tickles the back of my neck as the sun soaks into my bones, warming me from the inside out. I hear the gate click shut and turn to see John walking across the lawn. I shield my eyes from the sun and wave. My heart flutters as I stand to greet him. My view narrows for a split second, darkening the world around me. I steady myself and shrug off the sensation as a side effect of this pregnancy.

In one motion, John's cap is on the blanket and Calla is in his arms. She squeals in delight as he buzzes raspberries onto her pudgy cheek. Her cornflower blue eyes sparkle—eyes, John reminds me, that I was generous enough to share with her. John wraps me in an embrace before bending to talk to my bulging tummy.

"Lemonade?" I ask as I squeeze his hand. I head toward the back door of the little blue house we've called home since a few months after we were married.

"Please," he says. "Would you like some lemonade, too?" John asks Calla as she squirms and tries to wriggle out of his arms so she can climb the three steps on her own.

"Peeeze," she says, focusing on the steps before her.

I hold the screen door open and watch Calla's face, ripe with determination. "How was your day?" I ask John.

"Good. I finished up the Callaghans' cabinets today. They turned out mighty nice."

After leaving the army, John took a job building custom cabinets. His attention to detail and his eye for stunning lines has kept him busy these past few years. The Cedar Springs housing boom certainly helped, as military men returned home to resume their lives. The town now bustles as new shops and services open their doors to the growing community.

Calla waddles into the kitchen and settles her dolly on one of the chairs before climbing into her own. John stands close by, watching but allowing her the freedom to have her own accomplishment.

I tug on the refrigerator door. A knife like pain cuts through my middle and I gasp. I grip the fridge door with one hand and use the other to support myself against the counter. John is at my side with his hand over my back.

"False alarm, I'm sure." I smile weakly.

"Vi, are you sure? You've still got a couple months to go." Concern etches across John's face. "This happen often?"

"Only a bit over the last few days is all. Nothing to worry about. I've got a checkup next Tuesday. I'll speak to the doctor, I promise." Fully recovered from the surprise attack, I shoot John a more enthusiastic smile and pour three glasses of lemonade—two tall and one small.

***

a few days later, pain sears through me in the middle of the night, waking me from a restless sleep. I clutch the edge of the bed and groan loud enough to wake John.

"What is it?" His voice is groggy.

"Call your mother." I pant between sentences. "She needs to stay with Calla." I shuffle to the dresser, pausing with each fiery jab. "We have to go to the hospital."

By the time I've managed to put on a housecoat and kiss Calla goodbye, John is dressed and backing the car around. I spend a few minutes watching her breathe, marveling at the rise and fall of her tiny chest. *These moments will be gone too soon,* I think as I rub her cheek with the back of my knuckle. "Sleep well, pretty girl. Mommy loves you. I will see you soon."

Mother Smith enters through the front door as I grab my purse from the hall closet. "Violet, dear. Is everything all right?"

With great effort, I smile reassuringly and pat her arm, trying to squeeze past her before another contraction takes hold. "I'm sure everything is fine. A few early contractions is all. Best to get them checked out."

"All right, dear." Never one to hide her worry, John's mother is already wringing her hands. At times such as these, I wish my parents lived a might bit closer instead of at the farm. Still, I am grateful for the help and the closeness of family.

"I'm sure we'll be back in no time. Thank you for coming. John's put coffee on. Should be ready any minute now." I close the door behind me, and John meets me at the steps to help me into the car.

                                    ✳ ✳ ✳

he situation at the hospital unravels quickly. I am admitted, only to discover that my family doctor is away for the week. John is sent to pace the waiting room as a new doctor introduces himself to me. He confirms my fear that I am indeed in labor. A nurse helps me onto a bed as I try to explain that I am not due for another month and a half.

The doctor, with little bedside manner, replies, "I don't think your baby is too concerned about a due date, Mrs. Smith," before he turns and walks out the door.

The night is long, filled with contractions on top of contractions. I am barely aware when the sun rises the next morning, either lost in the frenzy or greedily trying to sleep during the calm. I move through the day, eating ice chips and begging for John. The pain does not subside. Instead it intensifies, bringing with it an ache in my heart I've never felt before.

The doctor checks in every few hours, though his demeanor does not improve. He advises me in a matter of fact tone that pain medication at this stage will not help my baby or my own experience in any way. He says I should focus on breathing and pipe down a little, as my groans are beginning to upset the other patients.

Another sunrise ushers in a new wave of intensity. I swear I can hear John outside my door arguing with a nurse, but his voice is soon forgotten as everything around me closes in and I drift off into nothingness.

*** * ***

*D*rops of moisture are falling onto my forehead, snaking past my temples and into my hair. My eyes open cautiously to the brightness of the room. A moment passes before I remember where I am. "John." My voice is groggy and weak.

"Vi. I'm here." He wipes his eyes, the cause of my wet forehead, and lowers his face to mine. His other hand is gripped around my own.

"The baby!" I cry out, searching his eyes for an answer.

"We have a baby boy. Vi, he's beautiful."

"He's all right? He came too early, I was sure…"

"He will be all right. He is smaller than Calla was, but he'll be fine." John gives my hand another squeeze before placing a kiss on my dry, cracked lips. "My worry lies with you, Vi." Tears rim the edges of John's eyes. "They say—they say your heart couldn't handle the strain. Jarred was born three days ago, Vi. The doctor said you wouldn't wake up."

I feel the heaviness pushing down on my chest. John's anguish takes up more space than the tiny white walled room allows.

"Jarred. A strong name for a strong boy." I offer John a weak smile and turn my face closer to his. I feel the hallowed edges of death creeping in, yet I am anything but afraid. "You'll be all right. The three of you, you'll have each other." The silence in the room is punctuated by each raspy breath. "And our families. Family is everything, John." I feel the air leaving my lungs. My heartbeat slows, feeling as if it will burst under the weight of each breath. "Do me something, John, will you?

A slight nod is his only reply.

"Tell Mother she was right. I'll not die of a broken heart, after all. My heart—my heart is so full it's bursting with love is all."

"Vi, don't go. You can fight this. The doctors are wrong, Vi. They said you'd never wake up and look at you now. Don't give up, Vi. Please, I can't live without you." John sobs, and a waterfall of tears streams down his face.

"These years with you." A broken cough escapes my lips, sending a violent vibration through my battle weary body. "And with Calla and Jarred. They were my finest. I've never been so happy. So loved."

"Me either." John rubs his nose with the back of his sleeve. "I love you, Vi. I'll love you forever."

"I've always loved you, John Smith. You were my dream that came true, after all." My heart echoes like galloping horses in my ears, drowning out all my senses. My half open eyes watch in fascination as my butterflies are freed from the cage that was my heart, stealing my breath as they flutter. John's hand clasps mine so tightly that I am certain his love will go with me, no matter where I go. I close my eyes and the brightness of the room fades to black.

WHAT TO READ NEXT

*L*ooking for more?

Subscribe to Tanya E Williams' newsletter and receive At the Corner of Fiction & History. This newsletter exclusive eBook is filled with historical tidbits and story inspiring nuggets. Sign up today at tanyaewilliams.com

*   *   *

WHAT TO READ NEXT?

The story continues with Stealing Mr. Smith...

Bernice wants what she wants and believes nothing should stop her from having it. John Smith happens to be her chosen escape from a life fraught with disappointment. She longs for a hero all her own and will stop at nothing to secure herself a place in life beside him. The fact that he comes with the baggage of two children and a past he refuses to speak of, has little bearing on her obsession. Bernice has set her sights on changing her name to Mrs. Smith, even if she has to steal it from a dead woman.

Get Your Copy Today!

* * *

I HOPE you enjoyed Becoming Mrs. Smith. I'd love for you to visit BookBub, Goodreads, or your favorite online book retailer to post a review.

Thank you!

ACKNOWLEDGMENTS

A novel is merely a story extracted from an overactive imagination mixed with inspiration from real life events. It is in the weaving of a story that an author is applauded for their work. This task, however, is never an author's alone. I may sit down at my desk in solitude and uncertain, but through each step of the writing process, there is a force of individuals behind me who make me feel anything but alone.

Many thanks to those who have supported me along the way. First to my beta readers. To Tammy, whose insight, creativity, patience, and friendship continues to inspire, challenge, and uplift me. To Stefanie, who knows no bounds when it comes to a willingness to help a friend. You are my beta reader extraordinaire (and friend) for life! To Jill, with an open mind and an open heart, you offered your time and thoughts to a less than polished work in progress. I do hope it wasn't too painful for you all.

To my advanced reader team. You are amazing. I am filled with gratitude for each and every one of you who has so willingly given of your time and energy as I aim to send this book out into the world. I could not have done this without your support so thank you, thank you, thank you, from the bottom of my heart.

To my editor, the incredible Victoria Griffin, without your keen intuition and editing expertise, I would still be bumbling my way through another draft, wondering how to improve the story. I am honored to work with you and I look forward to tackling the next story with your guiding assistance. To my exceptionally talented cover designer, Ana Grigoriu, though we are continents apart, you took a vision from inside my brain and made it real. A magician you are, and I am excited to see what you create for the next story.

To my parents, words cannot express the gratitude I have for both of you. Without your guidance, belief in me, insights, and love, I would not be who I am today. Thank you for continuing to give of yourself so that I may continue to grow. To my enormous extended family, though not listed by name, you are supremely important to me none-the-less. You have helped guide and shape my experiences over the years. Some I've known my entire life and enjoyed many a celebration with. Others I've come to know through marriage. Then there are those, I know only through black and white photographs and the memories of those you left behind. Each of you played a crucial role in my life and I am eternally grateful to call you my family. It is true, family really is everything.

To Ginny, your belief in my writing ability is contagious and in times of self-doubt, even I believed you. Sadly, I gained much insight into the experience of loss through your eyes. I would give back that knowledge in a heartbeat to have Uncle Greg here with us. Thank you for being open, brave, and honest. To Donna, thank you for always letting me ramble over tea. Your support and friendship in my life and in my writing continues to push me forward. I do hope you enjoy the story and sorry for having kept it from you for so long. To T2, your support, friendship, and encouragement were crucial to my taking the leap, literally and figuratively into this wonderful world of writing. To Kelly, you have a knack for knowing when I need to be on the water or in the forest. I look forward to many more days among nature with you, my dear friend. To Dee, though, I'm not certain if you regret saying those five little words to me over dinner one night, but you are absolutely right. I always have a choice and I will be forever grateful to you for reminding me to choose happiness for my own life.

To Kari, the wind beneath my wings, my friend. You believed in me, even before I did. Without you, I would A) quite likely have failed a course or two in high school, and B) would miss you, even if I had never known you. You are a constant in my world, my thoughts, and my heart and I love you to the moon and back.

To Justin, my first reader of almost anything I write. To have had the opportunity to watch you learn, grow, and become a kind and compassionate young man, has been the greatest gift of my life. Your sense of humor and your creativity bring me great joy and I wish only the best things for you in your future. I am truly honored to be your mom.

To Dave, my world is better because you are in it. Your love and support have sustained me in both challenging and joyous times. You are the first person I want to tell good news to. You are the last person I want to see before I fall asleep each night. You are both my rock and my soft place to land. It continues to amaze me that one person can be so many things to another. My best friend and the love of my life, I am the luckiest girl in the world. Thank you for continuing to believe in me. I love you.

ALSO BY TANYA E WILLIAMS

Stealing Mr. Smith

A Man Called Smith

All That Was

Welcome To The Hamilton

Made in the USA
Monee, IL
02 May 2024

57671705R00090